THE GREAT
MORTDECAI
MOUSTACHE MYSTERY

THE GREAT
MORTDECAI
MOUSTACHE MYSTERY

Kyril Bonfiglioli
completed by Craig Brown

The Overlook Press
New York, NY

This edition first published in hardcover in the United States in 2015 by

The Overlook Press, Peter Mayer Publishers, Inc.
141 Wooster Street
New York, NY 10012
www.overlookpress.com

For bulk and special sales, please contact sales@overlookny.com,
or write us at the above address.

Cataloging-in-Publication Data available from the Library of Congress

Manufactured in the United States of America
ISBN 978-1-4683-1221-8
2 4 6 8 10 9 7 5 3 1

From *An Envoi to a Projected Work*

And patiently, O Reader, I thee pray,
Take in good part this work as it is meant,
And grieve thee not with ought that I shall say,
Since with good will this book abroad is sent,
To tell men how in youth I did assay
What love did mean and now I it repent:
That musing me my friends might well beware.
And keep them free from all such pain and care.

I

A pair of knaves for openers

Trust me that honist man is as comen a name as the name of a
good felow, that is to say a dronkerd, a tauerne hanter, a
riotter, a gamer, a waster: so are among the comen sort al men
honist men that are not knowin for manifest naughtye knaues.
                        —*Sir Thomas Wyatt in a letter to his son*

'I wooden, Mr Charlie, I reelly wooden,' mumbled Jock,
moodily gnashing his toothsome way through the bunch
of grapes he had brought me. 'I mean, you know the aggro
you're going to get if you try to complete that projeck, if
you'll pardon the expression.'

I was, you see, in what Jock calls 'horse-piddle' – what
you and I would call 'King Edward the Fifth's Hospital for
Officers Who Cannot Afford the London Clinic' – and was
recovering from a trifling operation which is none of your
business. (Oh, very well, if you must know, I had been there
to have a cluster of haemorrhoids beheaded, which was one
good reason for having no appetite for grapes. The other
good reason was that I don't happen to like grapes, a fact
well known to Jock.)

Perhaps I should explain that I have a Fully
Comprehensive Accident Protection Policy which
guarantees that if anyone even looks as though he's going
to be horrid to me he will be cured of all known disease.

Permanently. The Policy's name is Jock.

Jock, in short, is my large, dangerous, one-fanged, one-eyed thug: we art-dealers need to keep a thug, you understand, although it isn't always easy to persuade HM's Commissioners for Inland Revenue that it's a necessary expense. Jock is the best thug that money can buy; he's quality all through, slice him where you will. When I decided to conserve my energy resources – who'd want to become fossil fuel? – and gave up art-dealing in favour of matrimony I tried to pay him off but he just sort of stayed on and took to calling himself a manservant. He is not quite sane and never quite sober but he can still pop out seven streetlights with nine shots from his old Luger while ramming his monstrous motorbike through heavy after-theatre traffic. I've seen him do it. As a matter of fact, I was on the pillion-seat at the time, whimpering promises to God that if He got me home safely I would never tell another lie. God kept His part of the deal, but God isn't an art-dealer, is He? (Don't answer that.)

Ah yes, well, I've introduced both God and Jock so I'd better start tidily by putting on record that my name is The Honble. Charlie Mortdecai. I was actually *christened* Charlie; I suspect that my mother was getting at my father in some unsubtle way, she was like that. He wouldn't have noticed, he wasn't good at jokes.

Yes, well again, there I was, in my valuable hospital bed, tossing back little shots of Chivas Regal from the bottle-cap while Jock tore juicily at the bunch of grapes already cited, which had camouflaged the top of the paper bag in which he had brought me the booze. Pray do not think that Jock had no stomach for the Scotch; he, too, dearly loves such fluids but would have been shocked if I had offered him a suck at the Chivas R., for he knows his station in life. He was, in any case, more concerned to persuade me from the perilous venture upon which I was embarking.

'Honestly, Mr Charlie,' he pleaded on, 'don't do it, I beg of you. It's bloody madness, you know it is.' He paced to the open window, sprayed a moody mouthful of grape-stones into the welkin and returned to my well-smoothed counterpane. 'Playing with bleeding fire, that's what you're doing, Mr Charlie.'

'Enough, Jock!' I commanded, raising a commanding head. 'I am touched by your concern for my personal safety but my mind is made up. I shall go through with this, come what may. I must strike a blow for the free world while I still have my strength.' My commanding hand strayed to the subject of our debate: the already thriving thicket of vegetation which sprouted from the Mortdecai upper lip.

My ravishing wife, Johanna, you see, had taken the opportunity of my hospitalisation to nip across the Atlantic Ocean and pay a call on her terrifying old mama, the Gräfin or gryphon Grettheim and I too had seized an opportunity; viz., to grow a moustache, thus filling a much-needed gap between the southern end of the nose and the northern ditto of the mouth. It was prospering well although it tickled a bit – indeed, no fewer than two of the nurses had assured me that it tickled quite deliciously. I had often longed for such a thing – yes, the moustache – and was devoting all my energies to it. Meditation and a high-protein diet work best, you may take my word for it.

'Well, Mr Charlie, I daresay you know best,' said Jock in glum tones which belied his words, 'but I wooden be in your shoes for anythink when Madam gets back.' With that he pulled the now stripped stalk of the grape-bunch from his pursed lips, looking for all the world like some conjurer extracting a small Christmas tree from a rabbit's backside, and rose gloomily to his great feet. I raised a brace of benign fingers and promised that no blame would attach to him; I would assure Johanna that he had fought the good fight.

'By the way, Jock, was it you who kindly bought those delicious grapes for me?'

'Yeah. 'Course. Well, I put them on your account at Fortnum's, didden I? They weren't half expensive. Very tasty though.'

'Yes. They *sounded* tasty indeed.'

'Well, I got to go, Mr Charlie, got a mate coming round to play dominoes.'

'Splendid, it will keep you off the streets. Enjoy yourself.

Having any trouble with the new lock on the liquor-cupboard?'

He left in a huffed sort of way. I fished out the pocket-mirror to see what progress the moustache had made since lunch-time, then rang for a nurse.

———————

During my last few days in hospital nothing much happened. Jock continued to smuggle in my whisky-ration; young nurses sneaked into my room for a tot when the senior nurses weren't administering shaming enemas; the Senior Consultant – a chum of mine – popped into the room to scrounge a tot himself (poor underpaid wretch, he probably had to drink cooking-sherry at home) and to urge me to give up drinking and smoking lest I should contract Art-Dealer's Elbow; birds jabbered outside the window at dawn (when do the bloody things *sleep?*); and colour television made the evenings hideous. I applied for permission to have my canary brought in but it was rated a health-hazard, so my studious brain applied itself to nurse-watching. I soon had them scientifically classified by plumage, habitat and ethology, as follows: the elderly, ugly ones in moult, whose only pleasure was the administration of cruel enemas to the root of the trouble, so to say, and who sniffed like aunts when they caught a whiff of whisky on my breath; the Roman Catholic ones whose characteristic cry was 'You may stop that at once or I'll tell Sister;' the very brightly-plumaged ones who chirruped 'Ooh, you are awful;' and the almost-pretty ones who only said 'Oooh!'

Time passed slowly and my moustache inched forth so languidly that I sometimes feared that it was losing its sense of purpose in life – but there came a day when certain tubes were uncoupled from undignified bits of the Mortdecai chassis and I was told that I might navigate to the lav under my own steam. As I tottered thither in an imperious dressing-gown I could not but notice an uncommon number of junior nurses loitering in the corridor and, it seemed to me, suppressing maidenly titters. A few minutes later I realised why.

Whimpering, I was helped back to bed while squadrons of ward-maids, helpless with happy laughter, moved into the lav with mops and buckets. Later – much later – I felt proud to have brought a little sunshine into the drab lives of those underpaid little angels of mercy; but for the time being I sulked.

Soon, though, all wounds were healed and I received my Honourable Discharge from the very Matron herself; she said, pronouncing the capital letters sonorously, that I had made a Splendid Recovery and that she heard On All Sides that I had been a Good Patient. She also hoped that I had Learnt my Lesson and would not, in future, come into contact with Damp Grass, which she assured me was the ætiology of the common or garden haemorrhoid. I started to explain that, if she was right, then the piles would have manifested themselves on my knees and elbows, but she gave me an Odd Look. I suspected that she was just hanging about in the hope of a handsome tip but I'm sure you can't tip Matrons less than a tenner, and in any case I knew that she probably owned shares in the lazar-houses and would get her slice from the dripping roast as soon as I had paid my bill, so I stayed my generous hand.

Jock had a swansdown cushion waiting for me in the Rolls – he had a wonderful grasp of the fundamental necessities of life, bless him.

II

A queen, a one-eyed jack and a wild card

They flee from me that sometime did me seek
With naked foot stalking in my chamber,
I have seen them gentle tame and meek
That now are wild and do not remember
That sometime they put themselves in danger
To take bread at my hand; and now they range
Busily seeking with a continual change.

Back at the Mortdecai half-mansion in the North of the
Island – sorry, I thought you knew I lived in Jersey,
Channel Islands – I was convalescing splendidly, mounted
on cushionry of the finest and downiest, kneading Pomade
Hongroise into the fruiting vineyard of my upper lip and
applying a little Cognac internally, when the door flew
open and a radiant Johanna (to wit, my wife) burst into
the room and sprang rapturously into my arms, uttering
many a glad cry – only to recoil instantly, giving bent to
one of those shrieks which only the gently-nurtured can
command and then only when they find their mouths full
of well-pomaded moustache. I have never quite known
what the word 'eldritch' means but there is no reasonable
doubt in my mind that eldritch is what that shriek was.
No Sabine woman would have got into the quarter-finals
that afternoon.

There followed what I can only call an Ugly Scene. She
began temperately enough by saying that the Surgeon

General of the USA had specifically warned the public against such defilements and that he could call on the support of most of the sterner prophets in the Old Testament. I put it to her logically that whereas I had freely given her my heart, soul, other assorted organs and all my worldly goods, I had never put anything in writing about my upper lip, had I? This reasonable argument did not sway her at all – women use a different logic from men, you must have noticed that – and she redoubled her Jeremiad, calling my lip-valance a social disease and drawing impassioned parallels with the Watergate cover-up.

Thinking to silence her into melting, wifely submission I swept her masterfully into my arms. This time it was my turn to recoil with the eldritch shriek as she smartened me up with a gently-nurtured knee in the groin. 'Don't you dare to point that thing at me,' she snarled and, 'If I ever wish to munch half-grown brambles I shall go and graze in Potter's Field,' and again, 'Go mingle with the pimps in the Place Pigalle, your face looks like a dirty postcard,' and, 'You look as though you were going down on an alley-cat.' Soon afterwards, bitter words were being exchanged. Finally she clicked open the diamond-studded cover of her Patek Philippe watch and said coldly, 'As of this moment you have precisely five minutes in which to shave yourself back into the ecology.'

I was not going to take that sort of thing from any mere sex-object, least of all the wife of my personal bosom; I folded my arms lordlily and favoured the ceiling with a stony stare. She rang the bell for Jock, who had cowered out of the room at the very onset of the storm.

'Jock,' she said in a kindly voice, 'is the lock on my bedroom door oiled; does the key turn freely? Good. Oh, and will you tell the maid to make up Mr Mortdecai's bed in his dressing-room, please. And I shan't be down to dinner tonight, I'll just have something on a tray in my bedroom. Thank you, Jock.'

'Oh really, Johanna, now look here ...' I began.

'I prefer not to look there, thank you. I have already

had a hard day. I shall take some light reading to bed with me. Like the airline timetable.'

——— ·— ·— ·— ·— ·—

It was the cook's night off – it almost always is these days, isn't it? – so when I strolled into the kitchen for a reconnaissance, it was Jock who was setting a tray-load of delicious dinner for Johanna: a nice, thick little *filet mignon* with sauté mushrooms, grilled and stuffed tomatoes and all ringed about with *pommes duchesse* such as I never tire of and side-dishes of *mangetout* peas and Jerusalem artichokes. I rubbed my hands: earth hath not anything to show more fair. 'Give madam *lots* of those carminative artichokes, Jock,' I urged. 'They'll do her a power of good.' He shot me a strange look from his glass eye.

When he returned from the grocery-round, I asked him casually how Madam was.

'Fine, Mr Charlie. Full of beans.'

'And soon,' I murmured spitefully, 'she'll be full of Jerusalem artichokes too, heh heh! But, more to the point, where is my dinner, eh? Or rather, *when*, what?'

'That *was* your dinner, Mr Charlie; Cookie wasn't expecting Madam back today, was she?' The saliva which had been so sweetly flooding my mouth instantly took on all the savour of a panther's armpit. My face, I daresay, grew ashen. Jock was at my side in a twinkling, forcing one of his famous brandy-and-sodas into my nerveless fingers. (The secret of Jock's famous b-and-s's is that he makes them without soda: it is a simple skill, easily learnt.) I swallowed the prescription and pulled myself together.

'Very well, Jock, tell me the worst. Have we to send out for fish and chips or, God forbid, to the Pizza Parlour?'

'Well, I got a couple of gammon steaks …'

'Hmph.'

'And some of them French mushrooms what I can't pronoun the name of and a few eggs …'

'Yes? Go on.'

'And I could sortie up some of them Reform potatoes, cooden I?'

'I do not doubt that you could, but all these kickshaws sound more like a light luncheon than a nourishing dinner for a convalescent. Moreover, I am, as you know, eating for two; this moustache will soon contract beri-beri if it does not get its vitamins. Is there nothing to precede this niggardly repast?'

'Yer what?'

'Sorry, Jock. I mean, is there anything for starters?'

'Oh. Ah. Well, I do happen to have a basin of me French pancake batter standing in the fridge but ...' I looked at him levelly. He looked back as levelly as a one-eyed chap can look.

'Oh, very well,' I said and tossed him the key to the cupboard where I keep the caviar. Jock may not be the tastiest evidence of Divine Creation but he yields to none in the matter of making caviar blinis. Nor the making of Pommes Reform, if it comes to that. My fortifying snack was marred only by the compassionate looks Jock cast me from time to time. These looks became even more comp. when he came downstairs from taking Johanna her coffee.

'Madam have anything to say, Jock?' I asked idly as I did a little housework on the moustache.

'Yeah. She asked me if you'd got rid of that excrement yet.'

'Surely she must have said "excrescence"?'

'Oh, yeah, maybe that was the word.'

I picked a pensive tooth.

'Look, Mr Charlie ...'

I raised the toothpick threateningly.

'Jock, if you are going to say "I told you so," pray forget it: the surgeon warned me against flying into passionate rages until I am fully convalescent. If you were going to plead Madam's cause, you may forget that, too. While I have my strength, no-one shall harm a hair of this lip.'

'Matter of fact, I was only going to ask if you'd like a spot of music to sort of put a lid on your dinner,' he retorted in wounded tones.

'Sorry, Jock. Yes, certainly, do wheel on some music, I dote on such sounds.'

Knowing my passion for Grand Opera, what the sturdy

fellow put on the turntable was his treasured 78 mph record of 'Chi mi frena in tal momento' from *Lucia di Lammermoor* – a rather shrewd selection in the circumstances. Now, my own recording of this is sung by Enrico Caruso, Amelita Galli-Curci and three or four other chaps but Jock's rendering is by Shirley Temple and S.Z. 'Cuddles' Zsakal. Jock, you see, has been hopelessly in love with Shirley Temple since the days when he was the youngest delinquent in Hoxton. The record or disc is tuneful, digestive and mildly aperient.

'Thank you, Jock,' I said courteously after he had played it twice. Then I shuffled off to bed, for my wounds still ached in the frosty weather and my moustache needed its beauty-sleep. For a bedtime story I took with me the illustrated edition of Klossowski's French translation of Li-Yu's infamous *Jeou-P'ou-T'ouan*, arguably the greatest pornogram in any language.

My choice of reading was an error, for the *Jeou-P'ou-T'ouan* is not conducive to slumber. Within an hour I was tapping in a tentative, *husbandly* way at Johanna's bedroom door.

'Who's there?' she rasped in unwifely tones. 'I warn you, I am armed!'

'It's Charlie. Your husband, remember? C.S.v.C. Mortdecai?'

'Have you removed that excrement from your face?'

'You mean "excrescence," Johanna, surely?'

'Do I?'

'Oh, *really*. Listen, Mae West has often stated that kissing a man without a moustache is like eating an egg without salt ...' Too late I remembered that Johanna never salts her eggs.

'So go look up Mae West,' she retorted. 'At least you'll have a waistline and age-group in common. There are frequent flights to the US of A; I have just been studying them.' She seemed to be trying to tell me something.

'Oh well, goodnight,' I said.

'Yes,' she said.

I stumbled back to my bed, a broken man.

III

Queen high backs into the game

Kings may hunt and choose their chase;
You that in love find luck and no mischance
Right well consider all my case;
I step but may not join the dance,
Love bid me strive – ah may I yet find grace!

Since earliest boyhood I have ever loved the truth, so I shall not pretend that I passed an untroubled, dreamless night. That last 'yes' of Johanna's had stung like any scorpion. I was therefore in no sort of shape to answer cheerily to Jock's goodmorninging, especially since the grey light of dawn told me that the time could be no later than 10 a.m., quite half an hour before it is possible for right-thinking men to drift to the surface.

'A Dr Dryden to see you,' said Jock. 'Claims he was your tutor at Oxford. Cooden get through to you because of the telephone strike so he come here all the way. Personally. Forced his way into the house by stuffing pound notes into me hand.'

I sobbed piteously, drawing pillows over my head, hoping that this might make the world disappear. Jock, who is usually all heart, drew them away and said that it was urgent. 'Says it's urgent' is how he deftly phrased it. There was nothing for it but to sit up and glare at the world through bloodshot eyes. The tea-tray swam into focus, followed by Jock.

'Jock,' I said, selecting the word carefully. 'Bring me the emergency kit. Five minutes later I shall have my French breakfast, after which you may produce this alleged tutor.' The emergency kit, thanks to Jock's insight, was already at hand: the Alka-Seltzer roaring in its glass, the half-tablet of dextroamphetamine on its own coy saucer, the vitamin capsules on another and the brandy and water beaming from a well-polished glass. After the decent interval stated, my French breakfast arrived: the big bowl of coffee so generously garnished with rum that only its fragrance betrayed the presence of coffee. With this came, of course, the hot-plate of anchovy toast – I have no patience with those weaklings who take *cinnamon* toast with their coffee.

Hard on the heels of this modest meal came Dryden, crying, 'Well well well, my *dear* Mortdecai! What a capital morning it is, to be sure!'

Try as I may, I have never devised a retort to observations of that kind, so I fell back on an old favourite which never fails to please.

'Yes,' I said.

Then I said, 'Have you breakfasted, John?'

'Well, yes, after a fashion. In Oxford. At *breakfast*-time. Then I had a cup of something nameless on Reading station. But be of good cheer, Mortdecai, your excellent butler is bringing me a proper breakfast presently.'

'Butler?' I asked puzzledly. '*Butler*? Oh, do you mean the big, ugly chap with one eye?'

'He is, indeed, a generously-built man and I fancy I detected a certain, ah, capriciousness in the collimation of his eyes but as to ugliness – who are we to make value-judgements of that kind? We cannot all boast of the symmetrically pleasing features with which you and I have been ...' At this point the words seemed to perish in his throat; he leant forward, pushed his spectacles onto his forehead and peered with alarm at my afforestation-area. He cleared his throat as though to speak but was rescued by the entry of Jock, who bore a tray loaded with all those delicacies of the season calculated for the latitude of breakfast. I freely admit to being a little miffed, for such breakfasts rarely come my way. Dryden, clearly, had laid out his pound notes to some profit. I could not bear the fragrance of the chops, the kippers, the devilled kidneys, the shirred eggs and the frizzled ham; I rolled out of bed and forced myself under the shower, muttering 'grnnghmphrrgh,' or words to that effect.

Mind you, a morning shower, especially if you are man enough to turn it to COLD before you get out, makes one superior to the lusts of the flesh; thus it was a superior Mortdecai who swept back into the bedroom clad in his costly Charvet dressing-gown ... no, wait, posterity must not be paltered with, I'm pretty sure that it was the costly *Sulka* dressing-gown that day. The bedroom was redolent with the fragrance of costly breakfasts so I opened the window in a marked manner before hopping back into bed.

'Now, John,' I said. 'Tell me all, omitting no detail however slight. Begin at the beginning and' – here I glanced at my watch – 'continue unto the very end.' I composed myself into an attitude which the ordinary housewife would take to be a listening one but which is also most conducive to light sleep.

'I shall be brief,' he began, in the firm tones of one who is good for at least an hour's orotund speech. (I may say that *Fildes's Donsform* never lays him at better than evens in the annual Lecturers' Puissance Trials.) 'Something quite awful has happened at Scone – and I am not one who lightly uses the word "awful." The Warden and Fellows are most upset. You remember Fellworthy?'

'No,' I said.

'Oh come, Mortdecai, you must remember her *vividly*: you and she Did Not Get On the night you met in the Senior Common Room.'

'Ah, you mean Gwladys, the she-don you elected a couple of years ago; I recall her now, she seemed as though she had been enjoying a difficult menopause since early youth. Yes, she is rather awful, I agree, but surely time has healed all wounds?'

'No no no, my dear chap, it is to her that the awful thing has happened. She is dead. Her motorcar came into headlong collision with one of those omnibi you see in the High nowadays. She died instantly. And her name was not Gwladys but Bronwen.'

'*Mors communis omnibus*, John, but how is this a matter for grief and for incontinent trips to Jersey? I mean to say, there is no world shortage of lady-dons, is there? They are like dragon's teeth, raze one lady-don to the ground and a dozen lady-dons spring up in her place, this is well-known.'

'You mistake me, perhaps wilfully, Mortdecai. The College is not greatly exercised by the question of replacing her – nor, I hasten to say, am I here to offer you the vacant Fellowship.'

'Aw, shucks,' I murmured.

'Nor, indeed, must I pretend that she had made herself wholly popular: she was not, so to say, the *toast* of the Senior Common Room by the time of her demise ... pray do not smirk, Mortdecai, it has a disturbing effect when viewed through that, ah ...' and he waved a few limp fingers in the general direction of my lip-garden, '... no, the core and centre of the matter is that, regardless of sex, creed, colour and affability – and here I speak for the whole of the SCR – she was a Fellow and Tutor of Scone College and the world must learn that Fellows and Tutors of Scone College shall not be done to death with impunity.'

The starter-motor of my brain was churning frantically and now a cylinder or two of the engine itself started fitfully to fire.

'John,' I said wonderingly, 'are you trying to say that you wish me to have the driver of the omnibus assassinated? This could, of course, be arranged but I must say that it seems an over-reaction on your part, not to say a fearful visitation on a bus driver for allowing his attention to waver for a moment; aye, and a bus driver who almost certainly has a wife or two to support. I mean to say, would you call this ancient, liberal and humane? What?'

'If you would favour me with your undivided attention for a few more minutes, Mortdecai, you would understand that nothing of the sort is dreamed of. No blame whatsoever attaches to the omnibus driver; he was about his lawful occasions when Bronwen, driving furiously on the wrong side of the street, immolated herself upon the radiator of his bus.'

'Pissed as a pudding, clearly,' I said, pursing my lips disapprovingly then quickly unpursing them on account of the moustache, which was stiff with its morning ration of pomade. 'Probably been dining and carousing at one of those women's colleges – hotbeds of alcoholism, everyone knows that. Send 'em all back to Cambridge is what I say.'

'Forgive me, dear boy, but you are in error again. The incident took place in the early afternoon and Bronwen had been lunching at one of those Turl Street colleges, famed for its stinginess with wine. Moreover, she was noted for her abstemious habits (we have ascertained that she had taken but one glass of sherry and one of Slovene Riesling) and was quite vexatiously cautious when driving. Nevertheless, all innocent bystanders agree that she started her motorcar, put on her tinted sun-spectacles and roared down the Turl like any Jehu, not abating her speed one whit as she turned the wrong way into the High, there to meet the omnibus – and her Maker.'

The Mortdecai brain was now firing on all cylinders, albeit a little raggedly still. I closed my eyes for a moment to aid the thinking process. Jock clumped into the room. I re-opened the Mortdecai eyes.

'Did you ring, Mr Charlie?'

'Eh? I? No. I daresay Dr Dryden did.'

'Ah yes, so I did, so I did. I was wondering, Mortdecai, whether this splendid chap could conjure up another of those richly-buttered muffins? Or perhaps a pair of them? Would that be a great imposition?'

'Cook's just starting to get lunch,' said Jock in his blunt way.

'Capital!' cried Dryden. 'For the oven-range will be already hot, will it not, and so the muffins no trouble?'

'Two muffins of the best and brightest, please, Jock; richly apply the very best butter and serve on a lordly dish.'

Then I said to Dryden, 'Was Bronwen subject to fits of ungovernable rage? Had she a tumour, perhaps, on the brain? Was she prone to epilepsy?'

'No, she had not the falling-sickness and her habit of life was so regular and unremarkable as to verge on the tedious. Until last week, that is.'

'You mean until death did her part?'

'No, no; she died early *this* week. I refer to the two men.'

'John,' I said patiently, passing a patient hand across my furrowed brow, 'I have been following your narrative intently so far and I'm prepared to offer you a great deal of seven to three that you have not yet drawn any two men into the sketch. What two men?'

'Well, you should really ask *which* two men, for there were two lots, each of two men, you see.'

I shut my eyes tightly and took a few deep breaths.

'No, I fear I do not see, John. For once you are not being your usual lucid self.'

'It is hard to pursue a rational train of thought in the midst of all these interruptions,' he answered petulantly, as Jock placed a laden muffineer before him. 'Thank you, my good man,' he added, 'these appear quite delicious.' Jock left the room, closing the door in a manner which made it clear that the pound notes were now accounted for in full and that calling people 'my good man' is usually reckoned an extra.

'Concentrate upon those muffins, John,' I urged, 'and collect your thoughts while I put on a clothe or two. I shall meet you downstairs presently.'

My head swam as I draped the lightweight heath-mixture tweed about my person and drew on the plain half-hose and the supple footwear. The tie which Jock had laid out for me seemed to have been hand-crafted from a richly buttered baby's napkin or diaper but I had to admit that it matched my moustache.

IV

Never draw to a pair of deuces

The Rocks do not cruelly
Repulse the waves continually,
As she my suit and affection,
So that I am past remedy:
Whereby my lute and I have done.

L uncheon is what we presently met at. I'll say this for
Dryden, neither pedantry nor paederasty had marred his
gusto for the more solid pleasures of the table; it was a
pleasure and a privilege to watch him ply the eating-irons,
his face as innocently happy as that of, say, Lord Snow
reviewing a posthumous book by F. R. Leavis. Jock, too, was
warming to the man, I could see that; he loves the sight of
a sturdy food-eater practising his craft and has often chided
me for picking at my food. Again and again he charged
Dryden's trencher with partridges and things, beaming at
the summary way he dealt with the polysaturated foodstuffs.
A *finale* of cold blackberry and apple pie was followed by a
coda of Limburger – enough to choke a yoke of oxen – and
a touch of my almost-best port.

At last Dryden tottered into the drawing-room and
subsided into my personal armchair, gazing benignly at me
through a poisonous Limburger haze. (I was rather glad that
he had polished off that cheese, for it is not so much a dairy

product as an instrument of biological warfare; it has to be kept chained down, and uninitiated guests have been known to ask pointed questions about the drainage system.)

He gazed, as I say, benignly and paid my household many a compliment. (Scone College, you see, is one of the brainier places in Oxford and the food there is correspondingly vile; I have heard that even Balliol dons blench when invited to dine at Scone's High Table.)

'Now,' he said eupeptically, 'where were we?'

'We were at a sort of crux, John. First you spoke of two men, then of two lots of two men. I long to know what you can have meant.'

'Well, Mortdecai, to tell the truth we cannot be quite certain that there was a *total* of four men, for one of the two pairs may well have been the same as the other two for all we know; you see that, I'm sure?'

'I am sure that I *shall* see, just so soon as you have told me all, in a sequential sort of way.'

'Ah, yes. Well, d'you see, Fred – you remember Fred the Lodge Porter?'

'He is etched on my memory,' I replied bitterly. 'Many an alleged race-horse did he recommend to me in my salad days and most of them ran like alligators in Wellington boots. Yes, I remember Fred all right.'

'Well, he is now Head Porter, perhaps as a reward for teaching so many young men the perils of the Turf. Be that as it may, soon after Bronwen's death he asked to see the Domestic Bursar and told him that some days earlier Bronwen had confided in him that she was beginning to suspect that two large men in dark suits were following her.'

'Wishful thinking?' I suggested.

'Just what anyone would have thought, Mortdecai, but Fred had, as it happens, been accosted in the friendliest way by two just such men in the White Horse tavern in the Broad; they treated him to a consolatory pint of ale after he had been narrowly defeated by the reigning champion, whom he had hoped to depose, at a game called shove-the-halfpenny. They encouraged him to gossip about his job and expressed surprise at learning that there was a lady-don at Scone and asked him many a question, plying him with ale. This puzzled him no little, for they were not, he is sure, policemen – chaps of Fred's kidney can recognise policemen, you know, however plain their clothes.'

'So can Jock. It is an innate gift.'

'He afterwards noticed these same men from time to time, loitering at a little distance from the College, sometimes peering into the windows of the bookshop opposite, as though enjoying the reflection of the College gates therein. He notices such things; he has been a servant of the College for many years now, man and boy – and the College pays its porters to keep their eyes open.'

'Just as we undergraduates used to pay them to keep their eyes shut now and then.'

'I daresay, it was ever thus. However, when he told Bronwen that he had himself seen two such men frequenting the neighbourhood, "she came," as he put it, "all over funny" and he took her into the porters' cubby-hole and gave her a chair and a cup of strong, sweet tea. She was, he says, "sort of pleased and frightened both."'

'That's easily explained, surely: she was frightened that she was indeed being followed but pleased that the men were real, not mere figments of her heated imagination. You see, women of a certain age live in dread of menopausal symptoms such as hot flushes and hallucinations.'

'Yes, that seems plausible, I must say. How I wish I had your wonderfully experienced insight into the minds of women; it would help me so much with the Brontë sisters.' I mentally sorted out some two or three rejoinders to that one but decided to let it lie where it had fallen. (Even had I skill with words I should not care to bandy them with Dryden; he once bandied several whole sentences with Bowra himself and emerged bloody but uncowed. His command of the subjunctive mood is a by-word in Oxford – for my part I never quite mastered the locative case.)

'As to the other two men,' he went on, placing his fingertips together so as to form a little churchlet, 'I have already hinted, have I not, that we cannot *assume* that they were the same as the first two, although they, too, were large and clad in dark suits ...'

'Yes, John?' I asked patiently, helpfully. His thoughts seemed to be far away. I brought the port decanter in and set it before him. He seemed to collect himself after the first sip or two.

'Yes,' he went on, 'the other two men – if they *were* indeed other – presented themselves at Scone the day after Bronwen shuffled off her mortal coil and showed the Warden some most impressive credentials. He is unable clearly to recollect the origin of these documents; I questioned him clearly but all he could swear to was that the men's authority appeared to come from the Ministry of Certain Things. I fancy he was jesting. He is, as you know, a Constitutional Historian by trade and much blessed with children: such men live in a world quite different from ours, quite different.'

I took a little port myself, to ease the throbbing in my temples.

'The Warden,' he continued, 'was enough impressed by these credentials to give the men permission to rummage Bronwen's set of rooms. They took away a suitcase full of her papers. The Junior Dean accepted what I would call a wholly inadequate receipt, written on plain paper and illegibly signed ... oh dear, yes, I quite agree, Mortdecai (although the phrase you use is strange to me), but we must be charitable; after all, if he were *clever* he would hardly be Junior Dean, would he? Eh?'

I repeated the phrase which he had found strange.

'One thing he did notice, though, was that one of the men spoke with a curious accent – American, he thought, or perhaps Australian or Swedish. Fred, alas, was not on duty in the Lodge that day so we cannot tell whether these latter two men were the same as the two he had met in the tavern, you see.'

'I see, I see,' I said, choking back another strange phrase, for the news about Fred's absence was the answer to a shrewd question with which I had been about to hit Dryden. No-one likes to have his shrewd questions still-born behind his front teeth.

'Are you quite well, Mortdecai? Shall I continue? Splendid. Now, you were about to ask me about Fred, were you not' – I ground a molar or two inaudibly – 'and then you were going to ask me to come to the point, to explain why the Fellworthy incident should be of sufficient import to impel the Second Senior Fellow of Scone across the foaming flight-paths to Jersey.'

'Some such thought did cross my mind, John,' I said heavily. 'I mean, even lady-dons have secret lives and strange accidents, statistics prove it …' He checked my flow of reason with an upraised finger far more minatory than I could ever command.

'Mortdecai, you surely recall that I was never one to use words at haphazard. I did not say "accident." I used the word "incident" choicely. The Warden and I are convinced that Bronwen's final, ah, *occident* – an elegant compromise, wouldn't you say? – was, not to put too fine a point upon it, bloody murder.'

I turned that word over and looked at the back of it. There was no solace on that side. I sipped a sup of second-best port; that, too, was thick and sweet as blood. Into each life some murder must fall but too much has fallen in mine – it follows me about like some blue-arsed fly but I have never learnt to live with it. Murder is for the younger set.

Before I could assemble a reply, Johanna swept in amidst a cloud of tourmaline mink. I presented John to her; she was wonderfully kind to him, said how nice it was that Charlie's old school-pals still visited him, hoped that he could stay for ages and ages then whisked away to her boudoir, leaving a ravishing hint of M. Patou's 'Joy' in the ecosystem and, evidently, leaving John Dryden a little squiggle-eyed. Before he could utter, I said, 'John, to tell the truth I usually have a little nap at this time of the day; settles my luncheon, d'you see. Daresay you could use a similar little folding of the hands to sleep after your early start this morning. Come, let me show you your room. Jock will call you at 6 p.m., when the life-giving drinks-tray manifests itself. Dinner's at eight, so you'll have heaps of time for your bath. Oh, by the way, we don't change here as a rule.'

'No, indeed we do not,' he said, wagging his head sadly. 'Except for the worse.'

'I meant that we don't change for dinner.'

'So did I, dear boy.' You see what I mean about Dryden as a word-bandier.

Having consigned him to his room and given him a couple of Enid Blytons and a Kyril Bonfiglioli to read, I stole into the dressing-room where I changed into my most fetching sleeping-suit, brushed my teeth and tippy-toed towards the communicating door of Johanna's bedroom, twirling my moustache and muttering many a 'heh heh!' like a Village Squire about to Have His Way with Poor Little Angeline. My hand was on the very knob of the door when I heard the key turn firmly. I, too, turned; first white with rage and then to my solitary bed. The illustrated edition of the *Jeou-P'ou-T'ouan* seemed to have lost its charm.

It is a terrible moment when a married man finds himself falling in love with his own wife; it's comparable with that traumatic moment at school when you discover that you are growing up and the masters aren't.

V

Two high pairs

What should I say
Since faith is dead,
And truth away
From you is fled?

For my part, I needed no rousing by Jock; we whose senses
have been honed to a razor's edge by the whetstone of war
can roll out of bed in one fifth of a second at the
lightest tinkle of a drinks-tray on the floor below.
Washed and dressed, I was offering the tall glass of iced
gin a perfunctory sniff from the cork of the vermouth
bottle just as Dryden staggered into the drawing-room,
fighting at the penultimate waistcoat-button. I poured
plentifully for him. Again he bagged my personal
armchair but I bore him no malice: a guest in my house
can have anything of mine. *Almost* anything. He was
giving me a detailed account of how refreshingly he had
napped, to which I was listening raptly, when Johanna
swept in, her lovely face just visible over a cumulus of
black diamond mink. She would not take a cheering
glass because, she explained, she was going to play
bridge at the Lieutenant Governor's and needed all her
wits about her.

'But I'm sure you boys can amuse yourselves, cutting up old touches about your schooldays together, hunh?' My old tutor made civil, puzzled noises; I ground a little more dentine off the molars.

'Oh, hey, Charlie dear,' she added, 'do you have a little cash money around? Just in case I lose at bridge?' Johanna never loses at bridge but I fished out my wallet, weeded off a couple of notes for myself and handed her the rest.

'Hey, Charlie dear, I shan't need all this; why, it must be nearly a hundred pounds!'

'It is precisely one hundred and seven pounds,' I said. 'Enjoy.' (What did she think I am – a Gentile or something?)

When she had made her exit and when Dryden had pulled himself together (he professes no interest in women but Johanna is something else again: she could have made Oscar Wilde sit up and beg) we turned to our drinks and to the matter in hand.

'You were about to tell me, John, your reasons for believing that Bronwen Fellworthy's demise was no accident. So far – pray tell me if I am wrong – you have evinced the facts that (a) this furious driving of hers was uncharacteristic; (b) two large men seem to have been taking an unnatural interest in her; and (c) two men, who may or may not have been the two already filed under "(b)", sequestered certain papers from her rooms. I agree that this is puzzling but it makes no sort of pattern. The Jehu-like driving might derive from a fit of pique at having been put down by one of the Turl dons at luncheon; the first two men may well have been private detectives hired by someone's jealous wife; and the second two may have been from the Public Record Office, searching for files she had absent-mindedly pinched. There is no case for murder, none. No jury would convict; no judge would hang a, well, a Liberal MP on such threads of evidence. Nor have you shown any Motive, Means or Opportunity.' I folded my hands complacently, wondering whether I should slip an airline timetable onto his bedside table after dinner or before. But he was no whit abashed.

'Oh Mortdecai, Mortdecai, you were ever a rash, headstrong youth. I recall the impetuous wager you made in connection with the seven nurses from the Radcliffe Infirmary ...'

'Yes, John,' I said hastily, 'but that was in another country and, besides, the wenches are dead, or married to handsome young doctors. More to the point, none of this is to the point, if I make myself clear.'

'Forgive me, Mortdecai, you are right of course; one should not "raise the follies of our youth to be the shame of age."' I had to admire that bit of in-fighting: only Dryden could so instantly have counter-punched with a line containing the dread word 'age.' I conceded.

'Pray go on, John. I am all ears.' He twisted the knife in the wound a bit by flicking a myopic glance at my upper slopes, as though trying to get a sight of the said ears through the tropical rainforest of moustache. I indulged him, I did not wince or cry aloud.

'You see,' he went on, wiping his spectacles in a disappointed sort of way, 'there is just a little more to it than I have so far related.' I screamed inside my head, for I knew those tones of old: they were the tones of a Fellow and Tutor who has something ripe and squashy up his sleeve. (I had last heard them a couple of decades before, when, as a second-year undergraduate, I was reading my weekly essay to Dryden. The subject was Sixteenth-Century English Prosody and, having passed the week amongst bad companions, I found myself with but half a morning in which to lay a learned egg. I sped to the Bodleian Library, as better men have sped before; found a relevant article in some obscure forty-year-old American Review of Renaissance Studies and copied it out entire. As I read it to Dryden that afternoon he appeared to be dozing at first, then heaved himself to his feet and roamed the room, taking out a volume here and there and saying 'pray continue, dear boy' in precisely those flat, silken tones to which I have just referred. I read on; he continued to fidget at his bookshelves, then – *joined in*. I faltered, breaking the duet. 'Yes,' he said, returning the book to its shelf, 'I remember considering that to be a rather sound analysis at the time. I wonder whether I might ask you to delight me with two essays next week? How kind. Good day.' You see the kind of contender I was matched against – a master of ring-craft. Rightly did the poet sing:

> Dryden, thou should'st be living at this hour;
> Cambridge hath need of thee, she is a fen &c.

But I am in danger of digressing.)

'Yes, just a little more to it than I have related,' he said. I recharged his glass. 'Thank you. You see, the Warden was dining at Corpus the night after Bronwen's demise and fell into conversation with old Schimpfen who was, nominally, Bronwen's Research Supervisor ...'

'Hoy, wait a moment, John; Schimpfen is Prof. of Mod. Slavonic Studies, surely? And Bronwen assured me, the night I met her, that her field was Sexual Sociometrics.'

'Very likely, very likely: she was fond of her little jokes, you know.'

'Little *jokes*? Bronwen? Surely it is you who are joking, John; la Fellworthy had about as much sense of humour as a prison door.'

'On the contrary; she had a marked sense of humour, although dry and unpalatable to many people, and her jokes were set to a time-fuse: like Edith Wharton's ghost, you didn't recognise them until afterwards. Naturally, this did not help to endear her to the Senior Common Room.'

'No,' I said thoughtfully. 'I can see that.'

'What emerged from the Warden's chat with Schimpfen was that Bronwen had quite ceased, this term, to consult with Schimpfen about her thesis, telling him lamely that she had become preoccupied with certain side-issues which had presented themselves during her work amongst the archives. She was vague and evasive about these but Schimpfen, who is by no means the drivelling old drunkard he pretends to be, formed an opinion that she had lighted upon something politically sensitive and was loth to discuss it with him. (He makes a great show of having no political views of his own, which means, of course, that he is either a Nazi or a Communist, does it not?)'

Having no political views myself, except a fixed belief that Attila the Hun was a milksop, I vouchsafed no more than a non-committal grunt. Well, I wasn't going to risk a *committal* one, was I? Dryden peered at me dubiously, then continued.

'The Warden, having mused furiously on this for much of the night, consulted with me the next morning. I urged him to take the whole ball of wax to the fuzz and spill his guts.'

'John, wherever do you pick up this thieves'-cant?'

'I believe I found the phrase in one of the novels you left with me this afternoon; it is the current *argot*, I understand. But now I come to the nub.'

'No, John, it is a quarter past seven; let us instead go to the reviving tubs, taking with us an ice-cold drink apiece. Jock will anticipate your every want. Our simple country pleasures are few, but the keenest of them is wallowing in a scalding bath enriched with rare bath-essences (I recommend the *Secret du Désert*), while clasping a thriller in the left hand and a tall, iced drink in the right. Tell you what, I shall even emulate old Ickenham and lend you my great sponge Joyeuse. Come.'

Stewing in my own juicy tub a few minutes later, I mused as furiously as any Warden of Scone whilst I soaped those parts of my person that I can still reach. Indeed, a passing window-cleaner might well have taken me for the very Master of Balliol himself, so deeply puckered was my lofty forehead. By the time that I was standing before the looking-glass, curry-combing the Great Bear, which by now almost concealed my weak mouth, I had come to several decisions, namely:

1. The circumstances of Bronwen's departure from this Vale of Tears were, indeed, indisputably niffy – and the 'nub' which Dryden had promised to relate would, I felt sure, only confirm this verdict.

2. It would certainly be my pleasant duty to give him of my plenty in the way of advice, counsel and admonition:

unstinted is what this advice, c. and a. would be, for my alma mater deserved no less of me.

3. However, any pleas for action, involvement, daring deeds and so forth were to be met with a firm *nolle prosequi*: desperate ventures are all very well for those who have neither chick nor child but I had a clear responsibility to my fledgling moustache – and there are no brushes, combs or *Pomade Hongroise* in the grave, we have this on the best authority. Had it been Johanna who had been zipped untimely, I would have left no stone unturned nor any avenue unexplored, but this defunct she-don had no claims upon my time; indeed, had her murderer entered the bathroom at that moment, blubbing out a signed confession in triplicate, I would probably have wrung his blood-boltered hand and asked him to stay for dinner.

4. Dryden, certainly, would grasp the opportunity of my well-known after-dinner affability to wheedle me into returning with him to Oxford but I would be prepared for this; wheedle as he might I would play the poltroon and plead many a call on my valuable time. 'Cowardice, be thou my friend' would be my watchword for the day.

I pressed the bell and when Jock appeared I asked him for a nutshell. He said that there was no such thing in the house, nor was there any point in sending out for one, since all honest nutshell-mongers would by now be caressing their wives behind shuttered shop-windows. It was therefore a merely notional nutshell into which I compressed the word 'NO.'

VI

Mortdecai turns over his hole-card

Longer to muse
On this refuse
I will not use,
But study to forget.

When I say that dinner was a tapestry woven by a great
artist out of every sea-fruit which Jersey can boast –
from *praires* to ormers to spider-crabs; when I say, too,
that this tapestry of finny and shelly-shocked denizens
of the deep was served at the table of C. Mortdecai,
then, mixed metaphors or not, I think I have said all. It
was a dazed and happy Fellow of Scone that I steered
into the drawing-room when the last curtain fell; he was
clutching a cigar and a glass of brandy such as few dons
can even spell, let alone afford. I was glad for his sake; I
felt that a solid post-prandial stupor would fortify him
against the trauma he was going to undergo when I
slipped him the contents of the nutshell. I, too, was in a
state approaching euphoria and quite prepared to let
him have his head in the matter of nubs. Since his
lucidity was once again a little scrambled I shall shake
it up and sort it out into a less garbled and more
dramatic form:

COP-SHOP, OXFORD
OFFICE OF DETECTIVE CHIEF INSPECTOR

(Detective Cheese Inspector is seated behind desk, up-stage centre. Enter Warden of Scone, prompt-side, down-stage.)

DCI: Ah, Warden, sit down, do. A cup of tea? No? Well now, to what do I owe the pleasure, as they say?

W of S: Kind of you to spare me some of your valuable time, DCI. I know you're a busy man so I shall come directly to the point. It's about Bronwen Fellworthy.

(Shadow passes across DCI's face.)

DCI: *(Guardedly)* Ah, yes; sad that, very. Yes.

W of S: *(Business with spectacles, notebook etc., then relates new evidence, summarised in previous act.)* So you see, DCI, that my colleague and I are now firmly of the opinion that this was murder.

DCI: *(Heavily)* Oh dear. Yes, you make a very convincing case, Warden. We certainly can't rule out Foul Play now, can we?

W of S: You will, then, be redoubling your investigations, no doubt?

DCI: Well, er. No.

W of S: Eh? Sorry, I thought I heard you say, 'Well, er. No.'

DCI: That's right, sir. My very words. Verbatim. As a matter of fact there will be no investigation whatsoever.

(Bitterness has crept into his voice.)

This morning I received a telephone call from Headquarters instructing me to close out the case. Since I did not know the caller I sent a telex to the highest echelon to which I have access, querying this astonishing order. I have just received a confirmatory telex phrased in a way which signifies that the order is not subject to comment and that I have no discriminatory powers in the matter. The signature, too, is coded to convey that the case is now under the umbrella of the Official Secrets Act, which means that I could be flung into my own nick even for this informal chat we are sharing.

(Flings meaningful glance at W of S.)

I cannot, of course, give you a sight of the telex ...

(Taps sheet of flimsy in centre of desk.)

... but that is the burden of its song, as they say. Now perhaps you'll excuse me for a second, I think I hear an unlicensed dog in the street.

(*Exit OP side up-stage. W of S dollies up to telex; reads.*)

W of S: (*Silently*)

OXLEADER YOUR EYES ONLY CONFIRM CONFIRM FELLWORTHY
FELLWORTHY MOTOROUT ACCIDENTAL ACCIDENTAL
FINALISED ACKNOWLEDGE YOUR DESIST SIGNATURE
STAFF MANAGER BOURNVILLE COCOA LTD LTD ENDS

(*Re-enter DCI.*)

DCI: (*Heavily*) While I was abating that nuisance just now, I picked up a message from the editor of the *Oxford Echo*. It seems he has just received a 'D' notice on Fellworthy.

(*Simmers, drums fingers on desk.*)

W of S: Look here, DCI, I don't know what the protocol is in your profession, so you won't mind my asking whether you would feel I was going behind your back or over your head or anything if I sought a confidential interview with the Chief Constable of the County?

DCI: On the contrary, I'd be delighted. Hope you can stir something up between you. As you can imagine, I don't much enjoy having the work of my Force interfered with by a lot of Whitehall washpots; it's enough to make an honest copper turn in his whistle and truncheon.

CURTAIN

———————

'My word, John,' I said when Dryden had drawn to a close. 'You promised me a nub and a nub is what you have delivered. Allow me to recharge your glass. Yes, if that isn't a nub then I am no judge of nubs. And what happened when the Warden saw the Chief Constable?'

'I do not know. The interview was to be at luncheon today. The Warden will, I am sure, tell us all about it tomorrow night.'

'Do you mean to say the Warden, too, is coming here?'

'No, dear boy, it is *you* who are going *there*, I thought that was clear.'

'Oh no it wasn't and if you want to know, oh no I'm not.' He gazed at me benignly, as you or I might gaze at a young moustache in need of parental guidance.

'But the Warden has *decided* that you shall, Mortdecai. He has his teeth into this matter now and will not lightly let go. Not only has one of Scone's Fellows been done to death, but People in High Places seem intent on whitening the sepulchre. He will not countenance this, for he has a tincture of Irish blood: in day-to-day matters he is the mildest of Wardens, but when that black blood of his is up, his strength is as the strength of, ah ...'

'... of ten, because his soul is pure?'

'No, I was about to say "as the strength of Miss Meadows's bed-cord" ...'

'Ah, yes; "which in dem day would a hilt a mule."'

'Precisely. After you have been, ah, briefed by the Warden, you will also learn puzzling things about Bronwen Fellworthy from the Dean of Degrees, the Chaplain, the Camerarius, the Domestic Bursar and the Fellow and Tutor in Comparative Pathology.'

'There is one flaw in your scenario, John. I am not going to Oxford this year.' My words might have been written in sand for all the attention he paid them.

'The Warden,' he went on serenely, 'asked me to think of a member of the College who was of mature years, not unacquainted with clandestine violence and investigatory techniques, not cramped by any too stringent a moral code and not likely to be recognised by one and all in Oxford. I thought at first of that chap who came up in your year, the one with the absurd Italian name, but the Librarian tells me that he has sunk to novel-writing and is living in syntax. Wouldn't do at all. Raffish, you see, raffish. So here I am, Mortdecai, here I am, bidding you answer the clear, sweet call of your alma mater, who will grapple you to her breast with hoops of steel. The airline timetable which you so thoughtfully placed on my bedside table tells me that our aircraft leaves just after luncheon tomorrow.'

I muffled an oath or two.

'John,' I said patiently, 'there are many reasons why I must refuse this signal honour; many. Foremost among them is the fact that my acquaintance with police investigatory techniques has hitherto been – to put it bluntly – from the customer's side of the counter. I'm sure you follow me.'

'Goodness, yes,' he cried merrily, 'we know all about that. Indeed, few men of pitch and sinew have not, in their youth, plundered a coy barmaid of her chaste treasure or pinched a policeman's helmet on Boat Race night. Such pranks are not held against us.'

'John,' I repeated, still patiently, 'I was not speaking of the deflowering of barmaids, nor of the unhelming of coppers. I was thinking more of killing chaps. Not once or twice but again and again I have been faced with the necessity of topping people, usually because they were offering to top me. Pranks of that sort *are* held against one. Forgiven, yes. Forgotten, no.' He boggled for a moment or so but stayed in the saddle.

'But is that not positively a qualification for the task?' he cried. 'You will be able to enter into the slayer's mind, will you not? Achieve empathy with him, forestall his every move, don't you see?' Well, of course, that kind of thing tends to put one into empathy with any slayer, however merciless, but I controlled my twitching hands. Scone could not afford to lose two dons in one term. I brought out my trump card.

'More to the point,' I grated, 'I am at present *in loco parentis* to a nursling face-forest which requires my undivided care and attention. You may have noticed it. My gardener has warned me that to ship it to other climes would cause what we botanists call a check in growth.'

'But don't you *see*, dear boy,' he cried, smacking a triumphant thigh, 'don't you see that this forest-primeval of yours – which I am sure is hardier than you think – is the very thing that the Examiners require? You will be able to walk around and about Oxford with impunity, the privacy of your features assured. Men may say "there goes a capital moustache" but none shall say "there goes a chap called Mortdecai." Unsightly though it be to the casual and undiscerning eye, it will be a positive asset to you in your task, nay, a boon, a fringe-benefit one might say, ha ha.'

Before I could summon up an adequately bitter retort, Johanna sailed in, radiant and desirable, tossing minks onto armchairs and pouring herself snifters of brandy. Any schoolboy would have recognised this radiance of hers as the radiance of a young woman who has just massacred a Lieut. Gov.'s wife at her own bridge-table.

'Charlie, you can have your pile back – whoops, sorry, I mean your wad,' and she slapped a chunk of currency onto the sofa-table.

'Are you sure that's right, Johanna?' I asked. 'I mean, it seems a trifle plumper than when I disgorged it.'

'It is precisely £33 plumper, dear. Since you were bankrolling my game I naturally cut you in at the usual 15% of the action. Well, goodnight now, boys.'

Dryden's lower jaw was resting on his breast-bone, his eyes were once again a-squiggle and a balloon seemed to rise from the top of his head, bearing the words 'SWEET SOCKO!' Before he could pluck out the Cupid's arrow which was protruding from his left pectoral muscle, I sprang to the attack.

'I'll give you my decision in the morning, John. Meanwhile, can I offer you a nightcap? At what time do you like to be called? The switch to the electric blanket is on the left side of your bed. The biscuit-barrel and the night-lights are in the pedestal-cupboard on the right-hand side. Beware of the carafe on the bedside table, it contains water.'

He took these delicate hints and the nightcap and soon we were toddling up to our respective beds, as sober as a judge. (You will note that I speak of only one judge; i.e. we shared one unit of judicial sobriety between the two of us.) Normally I would have urged such a guest to stay up until dawn, irrigating him with many an intoxicant and perhaps recouping my overheads by winning a few bob off him at gin rummy but I was by now concerned for Dryden's health:

he is no longer the don he was, however keen his mental powers remain.

(Nor would I have you think that I am one of those who sneer at senescence: why should I admire the astronaut whose mind has just learnt to conform to the mouse-maze pattern loosely called 'thought' and who assures us that the moon is knee-deep in dust and nothing else, yet scoff at the man sixty years older who has begun to discard the mass of mouldering luggage we call 'facts' and says 'I don't believe a bloody word of it'? Put it like this: if you were the Man in the Moon, and a spaceship – perhaps the hundredth such intrusion in the last millennium – clumped down on your territory, would you put yourself out to go and greet the idiots and meekly accept the regulation Hershey bar? If your territory happened to consist of valuable green cheese, wouldn't you arrange for a few feet of dust to be strewn over it? I'm not saying I'm necessarily right, mind; I'm just saying that explorers are usually quite as bad at their jobs as most people are. We still call a certain marsupial the Kangaroo because an early explorer asked an aborigine what the beast was called and the aborigine said 'kang a run,' which means 'buggered if I know, mate' or, in some dialects, 'I'm a stranger here meself.')

That parenthesis was really so that I could put off having to relate the gruesome incident which happened that night, an incident which scarred me as deeply as any haemorrhoidectomy. I was, you see, in my Village Squire mood again and was certain that this time I would Have My Way because Johanna, when she has just separated a few bridge-playing friends from their hard-earned trading-stamps, becomes suffused with marital affection, mere putty in my hands. I play on her as on a stringed instrument: it's something to do with bodily chemistry and red corpuscles, I believe. So, slipping on a suit of silken pyjamas and checking that all my own lance-corpuscles were on parade with bayonets fixed, I sauntered to the communicating door and rapped on it in a masterful way.

'Hmmmm?' she murmured in a mistressful, languorous way.

'Open the door, O moon of my delight,' I commanded, my voice husky with unslaked lust. 'I have come to carry you off on my milk-white stallion into the burning desert and Work My Will on you under the tropic stars. A groundsheet will be provided of course, for I know you are sensitive to sand in your, er, shoes. At first you may find the saddle-bow uncomfortable but you will soon embrace Islam, I swear it by the Beard of the Prophet!' (That sort of approach rarely fails to please.)

'Oh, Charlie, dearest, can it be …?'

'Yes,' I said in an even huskier voice this time because by now the corpuscles had broken ranks and were advancing in skirmishing order, their Tommy-guns at the High Port.

'… Can it be that our hearts beat as one, that we are twin souls?' Her voice was tremulous with womanly submission. I thought about the question.

'On the whole, I'd say "yes."'

'Oh my sheikh! My instant, vanilla-flavoured milk-sheikh! You are trying to tell me that you have scimitared off that Moustache of the Prophet, aren't you?'

'Er, well, not exactly. But I have rinsed away every trace of Pomade Hongroise and it is now a silken Perfumed Garden, redolent of *Secret du Désert*; you will learn to love it.'

A great silence fell.

'Johanna?'

Silence continued to fall.

'Look, Johanna, you know jolly well that you are the tree upon which hangs the fruit of my life. This is your own, personalised, sanitised Sheikh of Araby who seeks admission to your tent. You thwart me at your peril.'

'Get lost, Charlie Mortdecai. Go stuff a mattress with that thing. The moustache, I mean.'

If you are unclear about the precise meaning of the word 'aghast' you should consult an up-to-date Illustrated Dictionary, where you will find an artist's impression of a rejected husband with his left earhole glued to a keyhole. I considered asking her, in suitably strangled tones, whether she wanted me to beg on my knees but I realised that I already was on my knees – one cannot cajole through keyholes in a standing posture – and pretty soppy I must have looked, too. Well-nourished husbands in early middle age and silk pyjamas are not seen at their best when kneeling and pleading at their wives' keyholes, especially when viewed from a southerly aspect. I pulled myself together, made one last onset.

'Johanna,' I onset, 'you cannot deny that you are the wife of my bosom; you probably have a certificate to prove it, sewn into your stays. Shall the frail barque of our wedded bliss be shipwrecked on so small a reef as this scrap of shy moustache?'

'Yes,' she cried crisply. 'And it is no reef upon which the frail barque you speak of is foundering, the frail barque is becalmed in the doldrums of a Sargasso Sea of suppurating seaweed. If you choose to walk through life with streamers of Giant Kelp trailing from every nostril, well, that is a matter for you and your God to decide. What I have decided is that this bed is not wide enough for the three of us: that thing has come between us. I have been an indulgent wife; your Kermit the Frog is always welcome in my bath and your teddy bear has spent many a night under my pillow, beside my nightdress, but a line must be drawn somewhere and pot-plants are where I draw it; they have no place in the nuptial couch.'

I rose stiffly to my feet, for the draught through the keyhole was bitter. I did not vouchsafe a 'goodnight' for I knew it would only elicit another stinging 'yes.' As I crept into my narrow bed and reached for the latest edition of *Playboy*, I was reminded that Sir Preston Potter's immortal beaver was dubbed 'Love-in-Idleness' by the Master himself. I began to see the inwardness of that sobriquet.

VII

Dealer folds

But Lord how strange is this:
Once, as methought, Fortune me kissed,
Now all is changed that once me blissed,
For want of will in woe I plain,
I find no peace and all my War is vain.

Go burning sighs unto her frozen heart,
Lament my loss, my labour and my pain.
I see that she would have me slain!
Oh happy they that have forgiveness got!
Lo, this I seek and sue, and yet have not,
It paineth still: a wound from every dart.

Some officious early bird roused me from fitful slumber with its bellow of triumph at having lassoed a laggardly worm. (Try telling *worms* about the merits of early rising.) Billowy-bosomed Sleep, whom I love almost as much as twelve-year-old whisky, would not return, so I set myself to musing on the problems which had to be faced that day. I tabulate these, for my mind is tidy although my soul is a mess.

1. Johanna's proud spirit must be quelled; she must be brought to heel.

2. Since *force majeure* seemed unlikely to prevail (that knee of hers stings cruelly), the best course, surely, was to prove to her that the moustache of contention was not a mere toy but a precision scientific instrument: a thing of worth, a moustache with a mission.

3. Setting all that aside for the nonce, it was imperative to think of some way of gift-wrapping the ultimate 'NO'

which I proposed to issue to Dryden as soon as he had crunched up his Rice Krispies, his kippers and his richly buttered toast. This problem had priority, for if my presentation of the 'NO' was at all fumbled I would receive a reproachful stare from Dryden, carrying all the weight of vicarious stares from the Warden and Fellows of Scone College. Reproachful stares of that calibre are hell on the well-being of chaps recovering from minor surgery: my snip-cock or surgeon had specifically warned me to avoid such stares.

I mused despairingly – when, *when* was Jock going to appear with the tea-tray? – until, all of a sudden, a great light shone and I saw, as in a vision, all the bits of the puzzle falling into place:

1. I would quell Johanna's proud s. by stalking off to Oxford after all, nevertheless, and in a marked manner. No longer would she be able so cruelly to titter at a Mortdecai whining through the lock of an all-too-stable door.

2. I would explain to her, as to an uncomprehending child, that the moustache she had spurned was now about to prove itself as a necessary adjunct for a Sleuth venturing forth on a desperate mission, perhaps never to return.

3. Instead of turning Dryden's Rice Krispies to ashes in his mouth and receiving the dreaded reproachful stare in my natal stuffing, I could now greet him with a cheery and eupeptic 'YES' and urge him to try the cherry jam.

I checked the items off again, for I have never had difficulty in counting up to three, and the answer came out the same. There had been no flaw in my reasoning.

'Eureka!' I cried, just as Jock entered with the blessed tea.

'I *what?*' he asked. I fixed him with a keen, hawk-like gaze, such as you might once have seen darted from beneath a deer-stalker in Baker Street.

'Watson!' I cried, donning my new *persona* as the Master of Disguise.

'Well, *The Sound of Music*'s still on at the Regal, of course, and I think the Odeon is showing—'

'Very well, Jock; that will do. Let me put it this way: there is not a moment to spare, the game's afoot!'

This time he only gave me a pitying look and eased a cup of tea into my fevered fingers. As I inhaled the Broken Orange Pekoe Tips through my soup strainer, I fixed him again with the hawk-like.

'Have you your old service revolver in the pocket of your ulster?'

'Well I got me old Luger in the drawer in the kitchen table.'

'Then call me a cab!'

'Awright, Mr Charlie: you're a taxi.'

'How d'you mean?'

'Well, I couldn't hardly call you 'ansom with that bleeding moustache, could I?' With that he started to stagger about the room, helpless with guffaws and cannoning into pieces of fragile furniture as antique as his jest. The door opened and Jock's last guffaw was still-born behind his single tooth, for there stood Johanna, in thin array, after a pleasant guise, looking rather like Lady Macbeth on her first honeymoon.

'Ah! There you are, my dear,' I said, waving an airy teacup. 'I was just about to come and tell you that Jock and I are off to Oxford.'

'Oh no you're not.' I raised myself into a haughty sitting-posture and my tones became icy.

'Oh yes I jolly well am.'

'*You* may go wherever you wish, Charlie dear, you are your own master; but Jock stays. He has promised the Rector to give his well-known rendering of *On the Good Ship Lollipop* at the Parish Hall on Thursday. You shall not deprive him of his moment of glory, nor disappoint those of his friends who have been investing heavily in rotten eggs and mouldering oranges.'

'Oh, very well,' I said through clenched and smouldering teeth. 'Jock, I have decided to travel with Dr Dryden alone; you shall remain here and mind the shop. Kindly pack a light suitcase for me.'

'I already did that, Charlie dear,' said Johanna. 'Last

night. I put in that quaint old MA's gown of yours, was that right? Hunh?'

— - — - — - — - —

If the Good Lord had meant us to walk, He wouldn't have given us aeroplanes, would He, that's what I always say; but I sometimes suspect that He did intend *me* to walk – for the good of my waistline, perhaps – because every time I entrust myself to an airline something quite beastly happens, as though to rebuke my hardihood. On this particular after-luncheon flight it was a lightning strike of aircrews. The airline had roped into service a tumble-down old plane driven by twisted elastic, with a crew of renegade blacklegs to steer it. The Captain or driver, an ageing fatty with a Canadian accent, came into the cabin just before take-off to bid us welcome in person, explaining that he couldn't find the switch to the public-address system. He told us to be of good cheer, he had driven one of these kites before – in World War II. Blood ran cold in many a vein, but worse was to come: since there were no air-hostesses to be had, even for cash, no nourishing drinks could be served during the flight. Dryden and I look'd at each other with a wild surmise, silent upon a DC–7 in Jersey Airport.

The plane lifted off in a spirited fashion, the clatter of its elderly engines almost drowned by the buzz of prayer from those passengers who were not already occupied with the stout brown paper bags provided. The air was as full of pockets as a conjurer's coat and the fears of the timorous were not allayed when the Captain again strolled into the cabin, picking his nose and suggesting that it might be a good idea to keep seat-belts fastened throughout the flight. I paid him no heed, I had decided from the outset not to unfasten mine; moreover, I felt strongly that he would have been more usefully employed in his cockpit, watching the altimeter and ailerons and things of that sort. Dryden, meanwhile, had drawn out from the slot before him a tattered card of advice to passengers about life-jackets and passed it to me, making enquiring noises with his eyebrows.

It was in Italian, doubtless part of a job-lot picked up cheap after the War. He pointed urgently at it. The words ran 'La Cintura di Salvataggio se Trova Doppo la Poltrone.' I could not make him hear, for the starboard wing was screeching like a captive hawk, intent on Unilateral Independence, so I scribbled a free translation: 'The Belly-band of Salvation Finds Itself Under the Poltroon.' This seemed to give him naught for his comfort but my attention was elsewhere, for a raw-boned blonde in the seat to my right, her eyes clenched, had an iron grip on my thigh and was sinking a thumbnail in to the cuticle at every bump or lurch.

The next time that an idiot tells you it is better to travel hopefully than to arrive, you may tell him from me, with a full heart, that he should be posing for an illustration in a Manual of Gynaecology. Arriving is *lovely*, take my word for it, especially when the pilot of your aircraft has made three passes over Heathrow while he rummages for the undercarriage lever and lands at last in a series of frog-hops and a cloud of burning rubber. He was at the gang-plank as we alighted, becking and bobbing and hoping that we had enjoyed our flight. Dryden gave him a glassy stare; I shot a glance at the faded ribbon of the Distinguished Flying Cross on his breast. It was a glance that spoke volumes.

John and I broke into a dignified canter towards the bar but Fate was still tittering into its sleeve; an olive-hued barman eyed our progress narrowly and slammed the grille across his wares just as we were about to breast the tape. I'm sure it made his day.

The bus wafted us to Reading softly, speedily. (Why are airline buses so much better than airline planes? Why, *why*?) Dryden and I were almost reconciled to public transport until, at Reading station, we were decanted into the medieval squalor of a train – not the usual pigsty on wheels but a pigsty which had, that very day, carried a football-crowd. *Horresco referens.* Soon, however, the symmetrical Oxford gasworks hove in sight, then the propelling-pencil shape of Nuffield College, both breathing the last enchantments of the Middle Ages and promising an early sight of many another dreaming spire.

There was a taxi. It was not raining. At Scone we used the last of our strength to mount the stairs to Dryden's set of rooms, our withered tongues rustling inside our mouths and our courage sustained by the sure knowledge that gallipots of the pure, blushful Haig and Haig awaited us if we could but win our way to them. We burst in, fell upon the nutritious fluid with beastly snarls – Hogarth or Rowlandson would have whipped out their sketchbooks in a trice. We beamed at each other as our bloodstreams chuckled with pleasure like parched brooks welcoming a freshet.

'Now, John,' I said when the cacti had been rinsed away, 'as you know, I usually have a little zizz at about this time of day; you know, "Tir'd Nature's sweet restorer" and so on. Doctors recommend it.'

'And so do I, dear boy. Let me take you to your rooms. The Camerarius has agreed that you shall have Bronwen's set; I daresay you'd like to search for *clues*, eh? Ah, and this sounds like my scout – come in Turner, you remember Mr Mortdecai? – perhaps you'll be good enough to take him over to Ms Fellworthy's set. Nothing has been disturbed, Mortdecai, no-one has been in the rooms except a policeman looking for suicide notes and Turner changing the bed-linen.'

'And the two men from the Ministry,' I said.

'Oh yes, of course.'

'And the bloke from the telephones,' said Turner.

'Really,' said Dryden vaguely.

'Really?' said I interestedly.

'Turner will call you at six; we are invited to take sherry at the Warden's Lodgings at a quarter to seven. Have a pleasant nap.'

Bronwen's quarters were pretty Spartan except that she had evidently spent all her spare pennies on books: old and valuable leather bindings and new, expensive cloth ones were in great profusion. The only sign of feminine occupancy on the surface was a huge, pink, fluffy piggy-wig on the bed: a nightdress-case of the worst kind. Out of character, I thought; Bronwen had not struck me as a woman to be coy about her frillies. If any. However, at that moment I was more preoccupied with 'the bloke from the telephones.' Bronwen's instrument was of the newest variety, where you punch the number out with buttons instead of diddling a dial. My Army course on Hemiptera or bugs, twenty years ago, had not prepared me for such things. I undid it as best I could and studied its entrails but it contained nothing bug-like that I could see. What I did see, on the carpet below, was a shred of fine copper wire which might or might not mean something. Deciding to postpone my search in favour of my *cinq-à-sept* – for the most sophisticated bug could hardly learn anything from my melodious snores – I removed a few items of the gents' natty from my person and composed myself to sleep.

VIII

An open-ended straight

Deceived is he by crafty train
That meaneth no gile: and does remain
Within the trap, without redress
But for to love, lo, such a mistress,
Whose cruelty nothing can refrain.
What vaileth truth?

'Ha, Mortdecai!' cried the Warden cheerily as we were shown into the Lodgings.

'Ah, Warden!' I retorted wittily, surrendering my hand to his knuckle-crunch. (He is not a native son, you see, and no-one has explained to him that you don't shake hands in Oxford.)

'It is always good to see an Old Member,' he said, fixing me with his compelling gaze. I was in no sort of mood to be fixed with compelling gazes.

'Warden,' I said, 'you called me an Old Member when we last met, a year ago. I have spent much of the interim trying to decide whether this was a cruel jest or simply an unfortunate turn of phrase.'

'Ho ho,' he said obscurely, urging me toward the sideboard which groaned under many a low-priced bottle. 'It is uncommonly good of you to come to our succour, Mortdecai,' he murmured. 'These people will go at precisely 7.15 and then you and I shall have a Little Chat. Hmm?

51

Meanwhile, mingle a bit, eh?' I looked at the choice of mingle-worthies: it was the same mixture as before. One brace of second-year undergraduates who were being be-sherried for copping their Firsts in Honour Moderations; one All Souls pansy staring into his sherry-glass as though someone had piddled in it; one rancid portrait-painter on the make; one American Visiting Professor in a tartan dinner-jacket trying to tell risqué stories to one of those women you only find in North Oxford; the American's wife, whose dress had been designed in Paris by some poof with a keen sense of humour; a clever priest; an Astronomer Royal; and, of course, the obligatory black chap being courteous to one and all. I singled out the black chap to mingle with until 7.15 precisely when, sure enough, they all fled twittering like ghosts upon some dreadful summons. When the Warden of Scone asks you for drinks at '6.45 to 7.15' he bloody well means '6.45 to 7.15.' If you are still there at 7.16 he creeps down to his underground aviary and writes your name in a little black book, dipping his pen in bat's blood.

When we were alone, he fished a key out of a silver tea-urn and opened a cupboard containing much better bottles than those which were shaming the sideboard.

'*That's* better,' he said unblushingly as we settled into armchairs and sipped. 'Now, I understand from Dryden that you are more or less up-to-date about the Fellworthy business? John has explained all in his inimitable way?'

'I think so.'

'Did you ever meet her?'

'Yes. And frankly, I have to say that she was perhaps the only wholly unacceptable woman I have encountered in a long and varied experience.'

'Yes. That was not an unusual reaction to her lack of charm. Between ourselves, the Old Guard in Concilium voted her in *en bloc* just to teach us radicals a lesson, I suspect. Devilish clever of them, I'm bound to admit.'

'Yes indeed, especially now that her departure has been so unsavoury, if your suspicions are correct. As I'm sure they are,' I added, for Wardens of Scone are never wrong, even when they are wrong. Especially when they are wrong, as a matter of fact. I mean, can you imagine the Pope saying to his Cardinals, 'Look here, you chaps, I've been having second thoughts about this birth-control business ...'

'Well,' he (the Warden) went on, 'at the moment only you and John and I know all the grounds for supposing that it was no accident; a few of the others in the Senior Common Room know bits, of course, but I've asked them to keep mum. Which reminds me, while you're here you are a guest of the SCR; of course, sign for anything you want, I'll get the Bursar to settle your battels and other bills through the Eleemosynary Fund or something.'

'Most kind,' I said, a little stiffly.

'And I'll put it about that you're a sort of temporary guest Fellow, doing something vague in connection with our Police Studentships. Yes, sociology, that's the ticket; sociologists can ask all sorts of odd questions, no-one pays them any attention.'

'But *really*, Warden ...'

'Don't look so injured, my dear chap; all sorts of people are going in for sociology nowadays, it'll soon be quite respectable, just like economics was before Wilson. And it's only for a little while. It's what you chaps would call a "cover story" – is that the term?'

'I believe so,' I grunted, little mollified. He refilled my glass soothingly and led me into his private dining-room, where the sideboard was laden with many a succulent foodstuff.

'I thought that you might not want to face High Table food so soon after the fleshpots of Jersey – and you've only half an hour before the Duke's car comes for you.'

A lesser man would have lost control over the slab of game pie I was easing onto my plate. Jock would have said 'Yer *what?*' I only said, cooler than many a cucumber I could name, 'Which Duke?'

'Why, the Chief Constable of course.'

'Oh good; for an awful moment I thought you meant Marlborough. But I thought all Chief Constables were professional policemen nowadays?'

'They are, except ours I believe, and he's being phased out, so to say, as soon as anyone plucks up the courage to tell him. It's he that thought up and is funding these Police Studentships I mentioned earlier: we're making him an honorary Fellow and arranging a D.Litt. or something of that sort for him. As a matter of fact,' he went on sternly as he noticed my scornful eyebrow, 'he is not as ridiculously unworthy of such an honour as most of the analphabets we're obliged to give honorary degrees to; he's something of a scholar in his own right and extremely brainy. I suppose that's why they kicked him out of Trinity half a century ago.'

A bell buzzed on a desk. He spoke into one of those boxes you speak into. 'Thank you,' was what he said; then, to me, 'the car's here. Oh, and here's a letter from me asking all and sundry to be so good as to assist you in any way. Might prove useful. If any of the dons show coyness in answering your questions, just refer them to me. Goodnight and, ah, good hunting.'

The limousine was only, I suppose, the Duke's second-best Rolls, quite a year old, probably the one his wife went to the supermarket in. As soon as the ashtrays were full, he'd give it to his head keeper or a bishop or someone. Nevertheless, the radiator bore the ducal standard – furled, of course – and the doors were emblazoned with strawberry-leafed coronets. (Barons only have balls, did you know that? On their coronets.)

Wafted to The Great House as silently as the spicèd breezes blowing through a well-kempt moustache, I was admitted by a footman who smelled of *beer*, fielded by a butler who smelled of aftershave lotion and ushered into 'Is Grace's study, which smelled of the sort of cigar which Dukes alone can aspire to. A quite preternaturally long Duke unfolded himself from his armchair like a carpenter's rule; length after length clicked to the vertical until his gibbous forehead was swathed in the blue smoke which hung thickly at cornice-level.

He took one and a half paces towards me – call it nine feet and a bit – and repeated the name vouchsafed by his butler.

'Mortdecai,' he enunciated carefully, *interestedly*. 'Mortdecai. Mortdecai. How uncommonly kind of you to call, Mr Mortdecai. Yes, kind. Uncommonly. Are my people seeing to your horses?'

'As a matter of fact, sir, you sent your own, ah, carriage for me.'

'Did I really? How uncommonly ... that's to say, yes. Yes.'

Our chat languished a bit. He bent and peered at me dispassionately, as one peers at a peach which may or may not be quite ready for picking. I did not shuffle my feet – I peered back unabashed, for I have been peered at by Crowned Heads.

Suddenly he said: 'You'll forgive me for just a second, I'm sure?'

I inclined the head forgivingly. He strode to one of those boxes you speak into which have a sort of cowling around them, designed to let you speak unheard. The muffling never works.

'Secretary,' he said. There was a pause. His head appeared above the cowling, did a spot more peering, then ducked in again.

'Well, wake him up, wake him up.'

Another manifestation of the head; the sad, incurious eyes.

'Ah Johnson, there you are. Who is this feller Mortdecai? What does he want? Really. Indeed. Why wasn't I told? D'you think I should give him a drink? Seems a very odd sort of cove, just stands there, hasn't said a word all evening. Oh no, look here, you're not to sulk, you know how it upsets me. Good.' He strode back with a heron-like gait and loomed over me like a gantry.

'Water-bailiff,' he said.

'Not really, sir; more Mortdecai, to tell the truth.'

'No no no; it was the water-bailiff I had to speak to, about my water, don't you see. Fishing tomorrow. Hate it, if you want to know. Drink?' He shepherded me to a side-table and poured me a bumper of single-malt whisky with his own hands – I almost wished my mother alive again, she would have been so proud. (My papa was but a baron with balls on his bauble, she felt it keenly. The *disgrace*, you understand.)

'I say, do have a chair,' he said, looking wildly about him as though fearful that he had been burgled of all such furnishings. 'Now. This tiresome business at Scone. Had your Warden to tea this afternoon; jolly little chap. Ate nine cucumber sandwiches. Small ones, but still, very creditable, wouldn't you say? Like to see these young chaps tucking in, don't you? Well, now.' There was another pause. The desk-box buzzed. 'What? No, of course I'm not cross with you, Johnson. Now just you get your beauty sleep, you know how I hate it when you've circles under your eyes. Goodnight. No, I can't; I've got the water-bailiff with me. Goodnight.'

'Sorry, Mortdecai, damned water-bailiff pestering me again. Now; tiresome business at Scone, yes. Your Warden, you know, the cucumber sandwich feller, he's convinced that this awful woman-don of yours was done to death with malice aforethought and things. Can't have that. I'm Chief Constable here, did you know? Of course you did, of course. Forget my own name next; that damned water-bailiff. Upsets me terribly. Fuss fuss fuss. Moreover, the DCI in the city tells me that some nasty little Whitehall lackeys, "abominations of Moab" my DCI calls them, quite right, quite right, have had the damnable cheek to tell my men, not a damned word to me, mind you, that they're to lay off the case or they'll be bunged into the Tower. Shan't have it. Damnable little jackanapes.'

Exhausted with emotion, he lowered himself, yardstick by yardstick, into a massy chair with a strawberry-leafed coronet carved and gilded on the back. He had to sit askew to avoid the thing, squinted sideways at it as though he suspected leaf-curl. A door in the panelling behind him opened silently and the tear-streaked face of a beautiful youth appeared momentarily, then vanished. The Duke heard the latch click; he peered at me warily.

'Who was that, eh? Who was it, I say?'

'I fancy it was the water-bailiff, Duke,' I said.

'Damned fool,' he said obscurely. 'Now; as I said, I shan't have this impudent meddling from a lot of blue-arsed baboons in Whitehall, shan't have it. Do I make myself clear? Shall pitch in a really stiff Note to the Palace tomorrow; Elizabeth Battenberg doesn't like blue-arsed baboons any more than I do. Secondly, look on my desk if you'd be so kind.' I fetched an envelope made of the thickest, stiffest paper I've ever seen. 'That's a letter,' he explained. 'Tells people that you are carrying out some highly confidential enquiries for me. Says categorically that you're answerable only to me. D'you see? Good. Thirdly, you'll be so good as to call on the DCI at the Police Station in Oxford tomorrow; he'll give you a Special Constabulary warrant-card, you're to be a Special Detective Inspector with Detached Duties and you can draw firearms if you care to. Fourthly, that wasn't the water-bailiff just now, it was that soppy little rotter Johnson. Suppose I'll have to go up and say goodnight to him.'

He ushered me out carefully as though fearing that I might stumble.

To the footman (for the butler had dematerialised) he said, 'What's that on your breath, you rascal, what is it?'

'Beer, your Grace,' said the footman.

'Where'd you get it, I say where, eh?'

'Kitchen, your Grace.'

'Bring me some. I'll see this gentleman to his carriage.'

'Goodnight, Duke,' I said.

'I say, do call me Freddie,' he said petulantly, as though I were being haughty to him.

'Goodnight, Freddie.'

'Goodnight, sir,' he rejoined.

As we drew up to the gates of Scone, I passed a suitable gratuity to the chauffeur. He saluted as he opened the door for me.

'By the way,' I said, 'does his Grace keep a water-bailiff?'

'No, sir.'

'Goodnight.'

'Goodnight, sir.'

There were lights burning in the Senior Common Room; I telephoned from the Porter's Lodge and told them to send over a bottle of very good Scotch to my rooms. My bed had been made and the fluffy pink piggy-wig nightdress-case was in residence on my pillow. I went to the door and dropped the odious gewgaw down the stairwell, so that it would come to rest outside the scout's pantry, for I was in the high-handed mood of one who has just called a Duke by his Christian name.

'One of our better Dukes,' was my last waking thought.

IX

Player draws two aces

And better fee
Than she gave me
She shall of me attain,
For whereas she
Showed cruelty,
She shall my heart obtain.

C haps who have sipped with Dukes often forget to put
their names down for a cup of tea in bed the next
morning; this is common knowledge. I had forgotten to take
this important step the night before and Turner, the scout,
had not shown any initiative in the matter – perhaps he
had been unnerved at finding his pantry threshold
cumbered with fluffy pink piggy-wigs, who knows? At any
rate, I awoke at my wonted hour quite tealess. Showered
and shaven and unpretentiously clad, I shuffled over to the
Senior Common Room, there to cajole a belated breakfast
from an iron-faced steward. I still waken in the night,
quaking with horror at the recollection of that breakfast:
warm orange juice and cool coffee, dry scrambled eggs and
damp toast – but words fail me. I suspect the iron-faced
chap was trying to hint, ever so delicately, that breakfast is
not served after 9.30. My heart bled for my fellow Fellows;
what hardships the wretches endure in the cause of
learning, to be sure.

Not daring to ask for some healing brandy, I hastened back to Bronwen's set for a jolt of whisky to pacify my enraged stomach, then called on the Domestic Bursar, a genial old sea-dog who had scraped through to the rank of Rear Admiral without losing any actual ships and had taken an early retirement while he was still ahead of the game. He was reticent about Bronwen and a little wary of me – clearly, he was not *au fait* with the inwardness of it all – so I started again, by flashing the Warden's letter or ukase. When he did unpadlock his ditty-bag, he proved to be a mine of what might prove to be useful information. Bronwen, it seemed, when she first reported aboard, was in receipt of a stingily-endowed Fellowship, some teaching fees, a books-allowance of £40 per term, and the proceeds of eight University lectures, also per t. She had given every sign of subsisting on this income (which totalled per annum rather less than what a diligent dock-hand could make in a month); she wore the same baggy garments week in, week out, took all her meals in College, never tipped College servants at the end of term and rarely took shore-leave. At the beginning of the term before this one, however, the winter of her discontent seemed to have given way to a hint of spring; she was seen in a new tweed coat-and-skirt, acquired a small motorcar on the instalment plan and spent lavishly at Blackwell's book-shop. Latterly she had taken to having nice little dinners sent up to her rooms, and wines and spirits began to figure on her battels. 'And I remember the Dean of Degrees saying,' he said finally, 'that she had discussed with him a notion of taking a Sabbatical next term, visiting Poland and, er, that sort of place.' (He'd know about Poland because of its port of Gdansk – the other countries presumably had no coasts. Bohemia sprang to mind.)

'Thank you, Bursar,' I said in a brisk and seamanlike voice, 'that was most lucid, very helpful.'

'I see you're to be mustered as a temporary Fellow; mind if I ask ...?'

Well, I couldn't say it was confidential, could I, that's the surest way to attract attention and Rear Admirals are noted for their tittle-tattle and scuttlebutt, so I mumbled something about in-depth sociological on-going consensuses and gathering material for published work etc. This soon dampened his curiosity; he did not seem a *bookish* old sea-dog, probably spent his evenings curled up with an Admiralty Chart of the Falkland Islands. Or curled up *like* an Admiralty Chart, beside his torpid old sea-bitch.

For my part, I needed no charts; I set all plain sail for the shark-infested straits between Christ Church and Pembroke, on whose cruel rocks many a stout sea-don has left his whitened bones; then, dipping through the tropics by the palm-green shores of the Memorial Garden, I pitched up at the Police Station, where an Able-Bodied Sergeant piloted me to the Detective Chief Inspector's state-room.

A thick, hairy chap wearing thick, hairy tweeds rose from behind a telephone-encrusted desk and offered me a thick, hairy hand to shake. His manner was amiable – quite unlike the manner of the common copper of commerce.

'Sermon,' he said in a matey voice.

'Eh?' I said – for it was barely noon, not a time at which the brain is nimble.

'Sermon, Albert H., Detective Chief Inspector,' he explained. His voice kept its mateyness; he seemed to understand, from his wide knowledge of rats of the underworld, that some chaps are not at their brightest in the grey light of dawn.

'Ah,' I said. 'Mortdecai.'

'Eh?' he said, his merry eyes twinkling intelligently. I pulled myself together.

'No, not "A," sort of more "C" really,' I twinkled back. He beamed, moving his lips soundlessly as though memorising our little exchange for relating at the next Police Smoker. I could see that he and I were going to get on, that was clear.

'Now, Mr Mortdecai, I must ask you to do a bit of swearing.' I thought about this, shrugged a mental shoulder and offered a sample.

'*Bugger?*' I offered diffidently. He liked that very much, filed it away happily. Then he drew out a piece of printed card and told me to raise my right hand. I twigged, for I had been through this sketch at the outset of my brief and inglorious career as Queen's Messenger. I, Charlie Strafford van Cleef Mortdecai, therefore, did thereby solemnly swear to keep the peace in Her Majesty's Realms, to do this and that and to eschew the other. Oh yes, and I understood the Provisions of the Official Secrets Act and its Amendments, all of which had been read to me. I lowered the hand.

'Thank you, Inspector,' he said. I whirled around but found the office quite void of Inspectors.

'Inspector *Mortdecai*, I should have said. Here's your warrant-card, as per his Grace's instructions – and, may I say, with my hearty concordance and best wishes for a mutually profitable corroboration. Don't suppose you've a spare passport photo?'

'Sorry. And, in any case, I haven't had one taken since, ah ...' I gestured towards the 'fring'd pool, fern'd grot' on my lip, '... it's still rather young, you understand, too early to take it from its mother, really.'

'Not at all, a fine, sturdy growth I call it.' He pressed a buzzer and addressed one of his telephones. 'Artist. Now.'

The policeman who entered wore the pinched, bitter expression of an artist who had to wear his hair shorn to regulation length.

'Look at this gentleman. Got him? Right. Dig in the Lousy File, find a suitable mug-shot, touch it up to look like him. Right? Five minutes.' I gazed admiringly at the DCI; he clearly ran as taut a ship as any Rear Admiral or Bursar.

'As I was about to say, sir, you have my hearty good wishes and I'll be delighted to help you as long as you clearly understand that I know nothing about anything. That bloody Official Secrets Act is a bugger, if I may coin a phrase, and I've got my pension and wife to think of. You, however, have no connivance of the fact that the matter has been put under a bushel, have you, because I don't know what you're investigating for his Grace, do I? Now, how can I help you?'

'Well, I don't really know yet, Chief Inspector; I've only just started. Sort of feeling my way, really. I found what may be a bit of gravy in College today; I'll tell you all about it as soon as I've seen the lady's bank manager this afternoon. And I'd like to do a bit more poking about in College, too, while people are still remembering things.'

'Quite right, very sound technique. Which reminds me, the Chief Constable would like you to report to me – informally, of course, every day if possible – I'll pass him all the dirt that's fit to print. Verbally.'

'Look, Chief Inspector, I hope you won't take offence or anything – I mean, I'm just a novice, you know – but can I take it as read that the lady's corpse and car were thoroughly examined for signs of hanky-panky and what not? I mean, just so that I can rule out that sort of thing straight away? Sorry if that seems ...'

'Lor love you, sir, of course I'm not offended, you do right to ask. You know, the ordinary customer thinks that us country flat-foots sit around with our thumbs in our bums all day and have to scream for Scotland Yard every time an old lady takes a tin-opener to her gas-meter, but in point of fact we have a highly talented class of villain in Oxford. Some of the guests in our little hotel – yes, that's the local nick – are most ingenious indeed. I could name one or two of them who could steal your socks without taking your shoes off.'

'My word! But if they are so adroit, why are they in the, ah, nick, then?'

'Because we're better at our jobs than they are at theirs. But to invert back to your question; yes, we did indeed do a very thorough job on the *corpus delictibus* – our Surgeon is a zealous young chap, always looking for a Perfect Crime. If you chucked yourself off the top of a skyscraper he'd check for snake-bites and other rare vegetable poisons unknown to science. No, there was no trace of toxic matter discernible: he reckoned she'd taken one Feminax (that's for Period Pains) and about as much alcohol as you'd get in a spoonful of Buttercup Cough Syrup. We even took swabs from her eyes, what was left of them.'

'Her *eyes?*'

'Yes. See, some of our simple country villains here have noticed that you can buy a throat-spray without prescription which says on the label "avoid spraying near the eyes" – the active ingredient being benzocaine. So when they find some impudent outsider trying to tickle their slot-machine business, they fill him full of gin, give him a couple of eyefuls of the throat-spray, then put him on a push-bike – no lights, no brakes – and send him down Headington Hill in the rush hour.'

'God bless my soul.'

'Very likely, sir,' he replied enigmatically. 'As to the mortal coil of her car, well, they're never the same after headlong collusions with buses, are they? In fact, we had to extrapolate the wreckage into two unequal halves to remove the deceased, using oxyacetylene apparatus. But our Motor Vehicles Sergeant knows more ways of frigging with a car than you'd believe – he could make a fortune at it if he got bent – and he's pretty nigh certain that it hadn't been got at. Anything else?'

'Yes, Chief Inspector: are you free for lunch?'

'Afraid not, er, Inspector M. But if you still like the bitter in the Feathers across the road I'd be happy to join you for ten minutes or so.'

'Still?' I asked wonderingly. 'How d'you mean *still?* I mean, how do you know …?'

He chuckled fatly. 'Well, sir, that's where I felt your collar – apprehended you – ooh, twenty-odd years ago. Bonfire night. You'd pinched my helmet – I was a uniformed constable at the time.'

'Good Lord! Then it was you who …'

'Kicked you up the bum, yes sir. Well, you had been sick in my helmet, hadn't you?'

'I fancy I had. Oh dear. But surely I …?'

'Yes, sir; sent me a replacement helmet the very next day. About three inches across. Bought in Woolworths.'

'Ah, but …'

'Yes, sir, you had tucked a few quid inside; more than ample, it's always a pleasure to deal with gentlemen.' I shifted uneasily in my chair, for the old wound still irks me in frosty weather: it is no small thing to receive a policeman's daisy-root up the sump. He heaved a ruled notebook onto his desk and wrote the date in it, then, in a fair round hand, the words 'Four Large Whiskies, Chief Constable's Guest.'

As we rose to leave, the artist appeared with an astonishingly good likeness of my moustache. The DCI gummed it onto my warrant-card, thumped it with a stamp and handed it to me. As we left the office my eyes strayed to his feet; they were shod in light suede shoes with crêpe soles.

X

Player calls for a fresh deck

Where is my thought?
Where wanders my desire?
Where may the thing be sought
That I require?

By the time I had grown out of train-spotting, stamp-collecting and bird-watching, in the order stated, I was old enough to take up the study of bank managers. It is not a rewarding branch of Natural History because in England there is only one species: the English bank manager (known to naturalists as Palgrave's Golden Treasurer). Age and diligence may cause variants in weight, waistline and value of motorcar but the species remains *sui generis*, so to speak, and impossible to mistake. Irish bank managers, now, may look like bishops or burglars, Beatles or bookies, but the English bank manager looks like an English b.m. Stand him in an identity parade, clothed in prison garb (which he will probably be wearing sooner or later anyway) and the veriest housewife – nay, even another bank manager – will instantly pick him out as a Lord of the Overdraft.

Fortunately, they never read anything lighter than Snurge's classic *Short-Term Loans*, so my own particular bank manager is unlikely to give me a hard time for writing the above.

Armed with this early training, no sooner had I been shunted through the door inscribed 'MANAGER' than I had the chap behind the desk identified as the manager of that bank – Bronwen's bank. Since I was neither a borrower nor a lender he did not rise, nor did he offer me a cigar, and the brief twitch of his pursed lips was a smile from the very bottom of the discards. I took the chair at which he waved a pallid flipper and spread out before him my credentials. He looked at them with unfeigned disinterest; his conscience must have been clear that week.

He said that no, he didn't mind if I smoked. He went to a window and opened it; perhaps he thought that he'd scored. He moved well and lithely, I guessed that he had once been runner-up for the Junior Cashiers' Welterweight Cup. He was wearing stays and one of those moustaches that bank managers are born with. (Cleanshaven chaps who claim to be bank managers are always impostors, mark my words.)

He also said that no, he could not give me a sight of the Fellworthy Statement of Account despite my impressive credentials; what the situation called for was Letters of Probate. He enjoyed saying that. Dukes, Wardens of Ancient Colleges and Detective Chief Inspectors, he seemed to imply, are but dust under Moloch's chariot-wheels; to Rimmon they are chaff in the breeze. Letters of Probate are the only meat they crave.

I hastened to say that yes, goodness gracious, I had *scarcely* thought he would lightly betray such a trust, after all, I wasn't a bank inspector, was I, ha ha. (Did he flinch a millimetre?) Indeed, we could have had this chat, I supposed, at the Maison Française Garden Party next week, to which I happened to know the Warden had arranged for him to be invited (well, I knew I could fix that all right). His eyes gave off a glint, such as chinks in people's armour give off. I struck while the chink was open, saying that if it came to that we could have discussed it after dinner at The Great House next month (that was truly a whopper: no self-respecting Duke has even heard of Clearing House Banks, he deals direct with Fort Knox). He melted almost visibly; the trained eye could detect gobbets of molten manager oozing out of the fatal chink. Still breathing on his base little soul as on a platinum flute, I protested that, why, only the other day I had been saying to Lord Rumble of Colne (his Chairman) that British banks were quite as silent as any grave in Zurich (may God forgive me) and that I wanted no more just then than routine confirmation of what the Bursar had told me about Bronwen's academic grants, prizes and awards. The sources only – I had no interest in amounts. How the fibs tumbled out! And how intently he now listened!

I lolled awhile, watching him muse furiously, weighing his professional integrity against not one but two social triumphs. In the meantime, our moustaches were exchanging invidious glances. Professional integrity lost the day, of course – doesn't it always? – and he mumbled something into the acoustically shielded mumbling-box on his desk. In a trice or two he was handing me three telex print-outs with the smirk of a doctor showing you your Liver Function Test results, confident that you don't know your AST from your bilirubin. He was right, of course, for I am something of a simpleton (indeed, when I was a youth my parents so despaired of my intellect as to contemplate buying me a seat in the Metal Market or, if even that proved too demanding, putting me into Holy Orders). On the other hand, I do seem to have picked up a few scraps of knowledge about the bits of paper that bankers swap around amongst themselves.

One of the three bits of paper he handed me was a mere TTP (Telegraphic Transfer Payment) which stated, almost *en clair*, its message, which was to pay a sum into Bronwen's coffers precisely equal to what the Bursar had told me her Fellowship was worth per term. The other two were Tested Cables and I put a baffled look on my face and a hand into my trouser-pocket. I'm not nearly so disorganised as my friends think: that very morning I had snipped out all the lining of the said pocket, leaving just enough to clip a small ball-point pen onto, and had shaved those areas of the Mortdecai quadriceps which were within reach of the said ball-point pen. The bank manager may well have thought that I was playing pocket-billiards but in fact I was scribbling rapidly onto the smoothened thigh.

Prefixes were what I was scribbling.

Perhaps at this point I should explain about Tested Cables. (If you are very rich you can skip this bit; in fact you can skip it even if you are but a common or high-street bank manager or an up-market thief.) A Tested Cable is a way of shunting chunks of money from a bank in one country to a ditto in another. Most of it is a jumble of figures, known as prefixes, indicating, to people who know about such things, the country, city and bank of origin, then the bank to which the lettuce is addressed, the account number of the recipient and, finally, the amount of lettuce to be shifted. Some years ago a goodish bit of thieving went on: you got into a bank-vault (at night, so that you didn't have to hurt anyone except the aged night-watchman who had previously declared himself willing to be biffed a little for an honorarium of £500) and, just for the look of the thing, you nicked the contents. You burned the notes, didn't you, because most of them had been 'punched,' or perhaps you gave a few to people you had a grudge against. What you really wanted was a sight of a certain slim volume which lived in the vault – I don't think you'd want me to tell you the colour of the binding – so that you could take a few holiday-snaps of its pages with your Minox camera. You left the book behind, naturally. It contained the prefixes of all the serious banks in the world.

You had, of course, already cultivated the acquaintance of a rich chap who had a bulging account in, let us say, the Reichsbank in Tel Aviv and you had elicited his account number, who knows how? Then, on the pretext of spending a dirty weekend in Paris, you spent a dirty weekend in Paris and opened a bank account for yourself there. Back in London, you dialled yourself into the kindly Post Office's telex system and sent the Tel Aviv bank the appropriate jumble of numbers; nipped over to Paris and nonchalantly let them fill your attaché case with large, vulgar currency notes. Well, it's a living, I suppose; the only dreary bits are all that air-travel and the *sameness* of Paris whores.

By the bye, I really wouldn't urge you to try this particular caper yourself: banks aren't stupid, you know. They sussed this one out after a mere two years and a mere twenty million pounds or so; one or two of the victims, you see, had at last noticed that there were one or two noughts missing from the end of their statements of account. Nowadays, all Tested Cable Transfers go through a frowsty room in the HQ of the Clearing House Banks Association, where sits a proud, rat-faced man who is Told The Trick each day by word of mouth. He must never write it down, on pain of being banned for life from the moustache-wearing classes. 'The Trick' may simply be subtracting the day of the month from the prefix or adding in the number 69 or whatever. Most of you would hardly remember World War II, but secret agents morsing messages in those days always included a Deliberate Mistake, so that London would know that they were not transmitting a load of old moody at the behest of an Abwehr person who was courteously grinding the muzzle of his PPK into their earholes.

If you'll allow me to get back to where I was – in the office of Bronwen's smirking bank manager – what I was doing was keeping the baffled look pinned onto my map while scribbling numbers onto the Mortdecai thigh. All three of the absurd bits of paper had two prefix-groups in common; one had to be the prefix of this branch, the other must be Bronwen's account number. I recked not of these; the numbers I scribbled were the other groups on the two TCTs, groups which could only be the prefixes of the banks of origin. Finally, I gave the fellow an overacted 'I give up' look, thanked him courteously, flicked a pitying glance at his starveling moustache, left my cigarette just where it would leave a tiresome mark on his leatherette desk-top and made the sweeping kind of exit which only Mrs Spon and I know how to do properly. (The boy who makes my shirts has tried and *tried* but has never quite mastered it.) (The sweeping-out of a room, I mean.)

Back in Bronwen's set I stripped off all clothing from my southerly aspect and shifted my tum aside so that I could see the ball-point marks on the Mortdecai thigh. I copied the numbers onto a very small piece of paper indeed before scrubbing them off the thigh. Then I lifted the telephone and asked for an outside line, for I wished to dial the number of a venal bank manager I know in London. Then I remembered the snippets of wire I had found on Bronwen's carpet and replaced the receiver. I thought a stroll would do me good. First I strolled to the joke shop on the corner and bought a brace of those little glass stink-bombs, then strolled further until I found a telephone kiosk which had not recently been vandalised. Having got through to my London number, I browbeat my way through the usual succession of secretaries whose only function is to prevent people talking to people they want to talk to and, in about £1's worth of time, I was helloing the London bank manager friend.

'Ah, Dennis!' I said.

'Oh, Christ!' he said. 'You again.'

'No no no, quite wrong, this is not the Second Coming, merely C. Mortdecai. Look, Dennis, you remember that slim vol. in binding of a certain colour which you showed me that time we got sloshed at luncheon? Oh do stop groaning; just take a squint at it and let me have the meaning of a couple of groups of numbers, eh?'

When bank cashiers grow up into bank managers there is a sort of *rite de passage*, part of which is having to take a kind of Hippocrytic Oath that they will never use expressions ending with the word 'off' to customers. I fancy I tried him sorely on this occasion. Choking back his spleen, he told me in a level voice that I knew perfectly well he could do no such thing.

I said that I quite understood and that I'd enjoyed our chat and had he seen our mutual chum Oakesy of late. He understood: I swear I could hear the sound of a moustache being chewed. Our mutual chum Oakesy, you see, is a bank inspector by trade.

Someone once said that if you whispered 'all is known' into the ear of, let us say, an American Cardinal, he would hastily pack a few pyxes and monstrances into a bag, don false whiskers and call at the nearest travel agency. Your actual bank manager is subject to similar, if lesser, qualms. Bank inspectors are rather like the Police Force's 'Rubber Heels,' indeed they share the same motto: *'Quis Custodiet Ipsos Custodes,'* which I have heard variously rendered as 'We Cop the Coppers' or 'We Tell on the Tellers.' They hunt in couples: the junior inspector receives a telephone call at 8 a.m., telling him to meet a senior ditto at, say, Ealing Broadway Underground station as soon as may be. They meet; they solemnly initial a sealed envelope and open it. Inside there is a slip of paper saying, perhaps, 'Market Street, Eastbourne.'

At HQ, meantime, the Despatcher of Inspectors is cackling hatefully as he cuddles his *Bradshaw's Railway Guide*, for the train the inspectors will catch at Victoria has a restaurant car but it is too late for what British Rail jestingly calls "breakfast" and too early for a life-giving drink. Heh, heh! At Eastbourne, they stamp into the bank's Market Street branch, flourishing many a dread credential and reciting an Ogden Nash-like poem which goes after this fashion:

Keys,
Please.

Then they glance swiftly around to observe which cashier has gone green about the gills, which teller is slipping his pocket-money back into the petty-cash box and feeding the racing pages of the *Daily Mirror* into the shredding-machine, which assistant manager is sidling out in the general direction of Gatwick Airport. Although I have never, thank God, been engaged in the banking trade, my very stomach heaves in empathy with those venal varlets.

If it comes to that, I shouldn't much care to be an American Cardinal, either.

What I am trying to get around to saying is that the very mention of our friend Oakesy's name sorted out the thinking-processes of my friend Dennis almost instantly. He expressed an urge to ring me back in ten minutes but was my telephone *secure*? I made it so: the usual gaggle of ladies past the prime of life was glaring and gibbering into the booth; I dropped the two little stink-bombs, scrunched them underfoot and emerged, smiling sheepishly and examining the soles of my shoes, as one who fears he may have stepped in a pile of Sunday newspapers.

My little ruse worked; when I returned to the booth or kiosk ten minutes later there were no other clients. When the instrument said '*dring, dring*' I clapped a hankie to the nose, entered, and was tersely told that the prefixes I had cited were those of (a) the Fetter Lane branch of the Narodny Bank of Moscow and (b) a private sort of bank which concerned itself exclusively with the cash-flow of the F. Xavier Kleiglight University of South Wichita, Kansas, USA.

'Spray that again, Dennis,' I said, 'I think some of it went down my shirt-front.' He spelled the words out, then hung up without a friendly word.

My feet found their own way back to Scone, for I was wrapt in thought until I was awakened by Fred the Head Porter saying 'Horses, sir?' I realised that I was standing in the gateway arch, muttering 'Whitehall Moabites, Moscow banks, Bronwen Fellworthys, Kleiglight Universities' while ticking these off on a finger apiece, hoping that this would help me to see what they had in common.

'No, Fred,' I replied absently, 'not horses.' Like a flash he whipped out a newspaper, saying:

'In that case, Mr Mortdecai, I'll let you in on—'

'Stop it, Fred, I beg you. Here's a couple of quid, back the wretched slug of your selection for me, but do not tell me its ill-omened name; your horses are always too polite for my taste.'

'How d'you mean, sir?'

'I mean they always courteously usher the rest of the field towards the post.'

He was not hurt; you can't hurt chaps like Fred.

XI

Dealer suspects readers*

Farewell Love and all thy laws forever:
Thy baited hooks shall tangle me no more;
Seneca and Plato call me from thy lore,
To perfect wealth my wit for to endeavour.

I was half-way across the Front Quadrangle when I remembered, pirouetted through 180° and retraced my steps to the Lodge.

'Fred,' I said to Fred. 'About those two men in the White Horse.' He compressed his lips, shook his head.

'Sorry, sir, never heard of them. Warden's orders. Never saw no two men.' I flashed the Warden's letter of credence. He decompressed the lips.

'Describe them, Fred.'

'Big, heavy buggers. Almost twins. Looked like fuzz but not quite, like. Grey hats. Pale eyes.'

'Fair hair? Ill-cut clothes? Like Russians?'

'Never seen them with their hats off. Big, heavy coats, neat but not what you'd call fashionable. Talked a bit odd, p'r'aps, but you get all sorts here, as you know; bad as Balliol. Only Russian we got here is young Mr Ivanov and he speaks better English nor what I do.

---

* No, not *you*; 'readers' is a cardsharks' word for marked cards.

74

When he's sober; he's mostly pissed – we call him *"I've enough,"* har har.'

'Har har, jolly good. What did they call each other, d'you remember? Not, for instance, "Basil" or "Tovarich" or "Piotr Alekseivitch" etc.?'

'Well now, that's funny, Mr Mortdecai, now I come to think on it I can't recolleck they ever called each other nothing. Not as I can recolleck, no. Funny, that.'

'But interesting, eh? Well, let me know if you remember anything else, even if it doesn't seem important, eh?'

I was half-way across the Quad again when I remembered again. This time I hailed a cruising undergraduate and asked him to point me towards the Junior Dean. He in turn hailed another, as follows:

'Hoy, Angus, where does Little Noddy keep his pot?'

'XIV.'

'Staircase XIV,' relayed the first. 'That's over there, the one after XIII but before XV.' I thanked him courteously.

'My pleasure, Uncle,' he replied. That was another puzzle for me as I paced Junior Dean-wards; the youth cannot have *seriously* thought me his uncle, could he? I mean, my brother has neither chick nor child and I never had a sister of my own; although I've had a few other chaps' sisters, now I come to think of it.

Little Noddy proved to be a costive little booby with a bad case of blepharism and other tics: clearly addicted to the Solitary Vice. That was probably just as well, for he did not strike me as one to win the heart of a fair lady, to name but one sex. His breath vied with his feet as atmospheric pollutants. More to the point, he was a brimming beaker of non-information about the two men who had given him the receipt for whatever they had taken from Bronwen's rooms. Ten minutes of eager spluttering boiled down to the fact that he was pretty certain that there were two of them, and of the male gender. He showed me the receipt, which read 'Received of Scone College one case and contents.' The signature, as Dryden had assured me, was quite illegible. The date showed the number of the month before the day, which might be construed as non-British. Which reminded me:

'I believe you told the Warden, Junior Dean, that they seemed to have an American accent, or Swedish, or perhaps Australian?'

'Oh well yes I think I was a bit of a ninny about that you see I've been thinking it over and now I think but I couldn't be sure you understand that it was a Welsh accent perhaps though I'm not awfully good at voices but one of them said "*Ve* don't usually give receipts ..."'

'I see, that's how Welsh chaps speak, is it?'

'Well I don't honestly know really I don't think I know any Welsh people really do you I mean they left awf'lly quickly they seemed in such a hurry probably busy men I thought.'

I, too, left awf'lly quickly. My nose, usually sedentary, was fast becoming an unruly member; it seemed to be pining to return to the comparatively new-mown-hay effect of the telephone kiosk. Soon I was safe in the Bronwenry, having closed its door and filled a great tumbler of Scotch and ginger ale. I gargled happily, deep in an armchair, my feet on Bronwen's desk, admiring the effect of the sinking sun's mellow rays on the rich bindings and polished shelves of her bookcases. Very slowly, as I admired, one of those cartoon bubbles sprouted from the top of my head, with the conventional electric light bulb glowing inside it. The aforesaid mellow rays, you see, were at such an angle as to make the dust on the said polished shelves glow: one could see just which books had been taken out since Turner, clearly no zealous wielder of the feather duster, had last dusted. Now, no-one would have taken out and replaced any books since the two men had rummaged the rooms and if they had taken any out *they* would have taken them all out, if you follow me. I hastily – while the sun's position remained advantageous – plucked out the seven assorted vols which Bronwen had consulted, hoping that they might furnish some tip as to what had been occupying her mind in the few days before she underwent the Great Change.

The *Times Concise Atlas* opened readily at pages 32/33 and again at 52/53: Central Europe and Western USSR respectively. Not surprising, since the late owner had professed Mod. Slavonic Studies. Feuchtwanger's *Ugly Duchess* and Rebecca West's *Black Lamb and Grey Falcon*: they made sense but told nothing. Wodehouse's *Summer Lightning*: only proved that she'd had better taste than one would have thought. (Perhaps the fluffy pink piggy-wig was a sort of *joke*? Incidentally, it was on the bloody bed again; again I dropped it down the stairwell. Memo: tell Turner 'more dusting and fewer piggy-wigs is what this set needs.') Back to the books. A highly covetable early edition of Boccaccio with woodcuts: shouldn't be surprised if it inadvertently crept into my suitcase before I left. A recent Len Deighton thriller, in hardback no less: bedside reading, I supposed. Pinched from a public library but that didn't signify: lots of otherwise upright citizens believe that pinching books doesn't count. Last, a *Shorter Greek Lexicon* of Victorian date and in that hateful binding which antiquarian booksellers call 'ecclesiastical calf.' Some long-dead, luxurious undergraduate had told the binder to interleave it and the interleavings showed many a crabbed little notation. No use to me: I only know the first four letters of the Greek alphabet: the ones they mark on exam papers. (I was chiefly familiar with 'Δ' or 'delta.' That's the fourth letter, if you care.) As I gave the pages one more riffle before casting it aside my eye was caught with a densely-written interleaf. *It was in ball-point*. There were two more such pages. The Greek was neither the small, precise script of the sedulous scholar, nor the dashing cursive squiggle of one who writes it freely; it struck me as clear but laboured. Memo: have it looked at. Might be anything.

I called for Dryden on the way to the SCR and Hall; he told me in sombre tones that he had heard through usually reliable sources that High Table was to be regaled with fricassée of turkey that night. I blenched. He made us restoratives in the shape of a pitcher of Fried Fox, which is gin with both sorts of vermouth. I took the gentle old soul out to dinner at the Luna Caprese in North Parade (so called because it points East and West and isn't a parade, you might think, but in fact because Charles I had an encampment in those parts). Dryden proved to be a surprisingly deft spaghetti-twirler and, taking a line through this, I asked him how his Ancient Greek was. Once he appreciated that this wasn't a vulgar joke he vouchsafed that he had no command of that tongue at all. We washed down our *rognoni trifoliati* and *vitello alla Marsala* with at least one bottle of something red, then went back to Dryden's set and made more Fried Foxes and, to be frank, became a trifle whiffled. So whiffled were we that after a second or perhaps third pailful of Fried Fox we had sketched out an absolutely foolproof nineteen-point plan for setting the world to rights in a fortnight: the sort of plan that earnest freshmen dream up after two pints of cider. The first point, I recall, the point upon which the whole grand scheme pivoted, was that Dryden and I should that very night heave a rock through the Junior Dean's window.

The Night Porter came upon us crawling on all fours in the Garden Quad searching for rocks which might have been overlooked by officious gardeners and, far from helping us search, implored us to repair to our beds, moving us to tears with his scenario of what the Astronomer Royal would say if we woke him. I fancy he must have helped me to my rooms; indeed, I know it for a fact, because I was in bed when I awoke, you see.

'Awoke' is perhaps too flimsy a word: I was in fact wrenched from sleep by a frightful hubbub which led me to believe, at first, that the Yale–Harvard Annual Football Match had chosen Bronwen's study as its venue. My piercing shrieks brought an apologetic Turner into the bedroom; he had assumed, he said, that I was even then at breakfast and had seized the opportunity to do a little hoovering. (Why is it that technology which has put men onto the moon cannot evolve so elementary a device as a silent vacuum-cleaner, or, if it comes to that, a noiseless dish-washer, a hushed food-mixer? I suppose the answer is that women would not buy them: the housewife's axiom is that work must not only be done but must be heard to be being done and that the more often she can cause her snoozing husband to rise from his armchair like a rocketing pheasant, the more his heart will melt at his helpmeet's incessant toil on his behalf. Indeed, there's probably a fortune to be made by the first man to patent a really noisy electrical hair-curler or a rowdy automatic sock-darner. The whistling kettle has shown the way.)

Setting all that aside for the moment, the simple, two-point plan I outlined to Turner was that first he should give that hoover a decent burial and that second he should bring me a pot of strong tea. Not in that order, though. Anon I heard the tea approach, rattling hideously on a tin tray; I clenched my eyelids so tightly that their muscles must have stood out like iron bands as I groped blindly for the proffered cup. Curiously, I found myself incapable of grasping the handle of the cup with any sureness. Turner coughed.

'Excuse me, sir, but perhaps you'd find it easier if you took your pyjama-trousers off.' I unclenched one eye so as to glare at the saucy fellow but observed, to my chagrin, that my arms and hands were indeed swathed in pyjama-legs, while a tentative movement of the ankles showed that they, too, had made an equal and opposite mistake when they put themselves to bed.

'Turner,' I said manfully, 'I think I ought to make a clean breast of it: to tell the truth I believe I may have been a little worse for wine last night.'

'Is that right, sir?' he said – incuriously, for thirty-nine years man and boy as a College servant arms a chap against whistling with surprise at such statements.

'Turner, was I sick by any chance?' He looked around.

'No, sir. Not so far as I can see, sir.'

'Bad luck, Turner,' I said (for being sick brings a scout a £1 mandatory tip for a few moments' work to which he is well inured).

'And how is Dr Dryden this morning, eh?'

'Haven't seen him; he'll have gone off to Parson's Pleasure for his bathe before breakfast, never misses.'

'Good God.'

'Yes, sir.'

Fortified by the rich Indian tea, I made shift to unbed myself by careful degrees and to extricate myself from the gents' slumberwear. Then I sat with my head in my trembling hands, wishing that it would drop off and put me out of my misery. It did not oblige. After a while I shaved, rested again, dressed after a fashion and considered the tasks which lay before me that day.

First, unquestionably, a visit to the Buttery. A glance at my watch showed me that it would be open and soon I was picking my way across the lawn to its benign hatch, where Henry, the merry Buttery-hatch custodian, having diagnosed my condition as I wove across the Quad, was already decocting an Uncle Christopher's Hangover-Repellant, Patents Pending in All Countries. It comprises a pewter pot of the very best bitter, preferably a little on the flat side, which must be swallowed at one draught. If you can keep it down, you see, you feel wonderfully better; if you cannot keep it down, why, you also feel wonderfully better for the stomach-shampoo. Henry watched me narrowly as I gurgled.

'All right, sir?'

'All right, Henry.' He put away the enamel basin he had held in readiness. I readied myself for the next task of the day: the Dean of Degrees. I ran him to earth in his office, where he was staring with jaundiced eye at the University Statutes. He was an unremarkable man: when you have seen one Dean of Degrees you have seen them all. Deans of Degrees lead simple, undemanding lives; their duties are curious but few. Each Michaelmas Term they lead a crocodile of freshmen to where the Vice-Chancellor hoves; the latter tells them in polished Latin that they are now matriculated into the bosom of the University and had better watch their step. Nine terms later he takes the same young men, or such of them as have stayed the course, to that year's Vice-Chancellor (one year of Vice-Chancelling is reckoned to be the maximum dose for an adult) and, holding them by the hands (yes, truly) he Supplicates that they be admitted to the Degree of Bachelor and allowed to wear a rabbit-skin hood. Yet nine more terms later, any of the same now not quite so young men who have clean noses and a clean slate at the Buttery are again led before the latest Vice-Chancellor who courteously removes his 'square' or mortar-board, administers another dose of Latin and zaps them gently on the noggin with a Bible, thus entitling them to wear a much richer gown, a red silk hood and the right to vote for the office of Professor of Poetry. During this ceremony it is the embarrassing task of the Senior and Junior Proctors to float up and down the aisle of the Sheldonian so that, theoretically, any Oxford burgess or tradesman can tug at their flowing gowns and forbid the banns, as it were, of any would-be Master of Arts who has flagitiously failed to pay his vintner, tailor or horse-holder.

The Dean of Degrees presently under advisement was clearly resting after the emotional wracking of last Michaelmas Term and recruiting his strength for next Michaelmas Term. Nor was he of any great help to me. He admitted listlessly that he had given Bronwen a provisional OK to her proposed sabbatical term but he didn't think she had made any firm arrangements with a Continental university, she hadn't seemed to have shopped around at the time. He had no knowledge of any extraneous academic grants she might have enjoyed but when I prompted him he sort of remembered that three terms ago he had written a letter for her to some extraordinary American place, declaring that she had a brace of degrees and was in good standing at Scone. Yes, 'Kleiglight' and 'Wichita' rang a bit of a bell, that would have been the place. As a matter of fact he remembered enclosing a declaration from the Chaplain to the effect that Bronwen was a practising Protestant, which may very well have been the truth for all he knew. I left the care-worn fellow to his onerous task.

I was a little stronger on the wing by now; I made it to the Library without difficulty and winkled out the Protobibliothecarius or librarian, who is a good egg and considers me to be pretty farm-fresh myself. He hoisted a monstrous tome called *The World of Learning* onto his desk and quickly snared the entry for the F. Xavier Kleiglight Univ. of S. Wichita, Kansas, USA, for there really was such a place, it seemed. Founded in 1936 and richly endowed by the mourning relict of F.X.K., it offered degree courses in Divinity of the Episcopalian or Protestant flavour (judging by his names, Protestantism must have been old F.X.K.'s third and last shot at salvation) and also had in its gift or advowson some fat post-graduate grants for research at doctoral level into Industrial Glues and Modern European Church History.

'Bizarre, wouldn't you say?' I asked.

'Not specially, Charlie. There's a place in Canada which spends fortunes on Creation-Myths of the Prehistoric Esquimaux.'

'How the other half does live, to be sure. Did you know Bronwen at all well? No, I suppose you wouldn't. D'you recall her ever asking you for the latest titles concerning Industrial Glues? No? Then it must be the Mod. Ch. Hist. Bizarre, as I said. See you at dinner tonight?'

'Not bleeding likely; they can't make me swill that garbage, I've got a Doctor's Certificate for duodeno-something or other.'

'And, of course, you're a Papist, aren't you, so they can't rope you into Chapel, either. I dunno, some of you dons seem to live for pleasure alone. Come and have a drink, it's nearly lunch-time.'

A brace of drinks later I felt sturdy enough to face luncheon: even Scone's College Chef, I reasoned, could hardly spoil Dover Sole and *pommes frites*. I proved to be wrong, of course – when, *when* will I ever learn?

XII

Dealer's choice: seven-card stud

When fortune gave good wind unto my sail,
Lo! Then of friends I had no little number:
But a squall arose and fortune 'gan to fail;
Adversity blew my friends and me asunder;
Amidst the sea, my ship was all too shaken,
And I of friends and fortune clean forsaken.

Crammed with distressful fish and chips, I collected the *Shorter Greek Lexicon* from my rooms, gargled with a little Scotch in case of salmonella or other food-poisoning and went in search of the Gulbenkian Professor of Greek Palaeography and Ancient History who happened – indeed, probably still happens – to be a Fellow of Scone. I had telephoned; he had admitted that he was in and that he could spare me ten measured minutes of his valuable time.

Now, setting aside such trumpery gewgaws as bank managers wear on their smirking lips, there are two major classes of moustache that need to be taken into consideration: the dashing, trendy, vigorous kind such as I was fostering, and the grand old timeless classics; massive, drooping patriarchs which have seen the clean-shaven fads come and go 'in patient, calm disdain – They watched the Legions thunder past, then sank in sleep again.' Professor Weiss's face was inhabited by a moustache of the second category, except that no Legion, not even

Ulpia Victrix itself, could have thundered through it without the use of machetes, pangas and other jungle-clearing implements whose names I forget. From the outset it made it clear that it was not going to take any impudence from my young upstart; it rustled threateningly against Weiss's very collar until my amateur orchidarium wilted into a sulky sort of deference, then it whiffled benignly as if to say 'persevere, young feller-me-lad, soak up all your nice, nourishing soup and one day you, too, will be a credit to your sire and this University.'

Precedence, protocol and pecking-order thus established, he parted the rich draperies from his mouth (the ungarnished mouth disappointed; it was pink and petite, quite unworthy of its princely pelmet) and uttered.

'Ah,' he said with his mouth. 'You are Mr er ah um, what?'

'Just so, Professor. Very kind of you to remember me.'

'And you were up here at Scone, were you not, in er ah um ...?'

'Yes.' He pretended to make a note in his journal and, who knows, perhaps he did. I warned myself not to take him too readily for a cloth-head, bluffing his way through academic life by virtue of a moustache; there are people of a certain kind of brilliance who choose to defend themselves against merely clever people by radiating daftness. Brilliant people never have to worry about their abilities: it is not the kind of thing we – sorry, I mean *they* – ever question. Daft people are like them in this respect. It is only the merely clever chaps like you and me who munch our fingernails to the quick, agonising over their placing in the 1 to 10 scale from 'smart-arse' to 'Vice-Presidential material' (that's reading downwards, of course, from top to bottom).

'You'll take a glass of sherry, won't you, Mr er ah um, eh?'

I agreed that his forecast was correct. He rummaged for sherry without enthusiasm and unabashedly confessed – or pretended – that he could find none. I fumbled with my cigarettes and lighter in an enquiring sort of way but this was met with a flat glare of such malevolence that cigarette-case and lighter seemed to leap back into my pocket as though of their own volition. He then proceeded to ignite, with every sign of extravagant relish, the foulest-smelling pipe I have ever sat across a desk from, and huffed and chuffed vile fumes across at me so vehemently that his great moustache cracked and snapped like a ring-master's whip. I am a man of much humility, as you must by now have guessed, and in my time I have been put down by far more hateful Professors of Greek Palaeography – aye, and of Ancient History, too – but I confess I was ashamed that my moustache should have had to witness such a second humiliation.

The incivilities completed, I proffered the interleaved *Lexicon*, which he accepted between knobbly fingertips as though it were the corpse of some small, inedible animal, rich in fleas.

'Beastly binding,' he grunted after a while, 'what they used to call "ecclesiastical calf," blind-tooled, with Oxford corners.' Well, I knew that. 'Printed at Leyden in 1845; bound and interleaved in Oxford some thirty years later.' I could have told him that, too, for I read print like a native, but I held my tongue. 'Not of the least value to a collector, nor as a reference work, but I daresay a bookseller would give you a pound for it.' I went on holding the tongue but the effort was great.

You must have come across those sad smokers who put their spent matches back into the box. They rationalise about it, mouthing rare words like 'ecology' but any psychiatrist worth his gestalt knows jolly well that it is a symbolic hoarding of the faeces and that the hoarder, fumbling amongst the grotty detritus to find an unused match, derives an intense if unconscious pleasure from this dirtying of the fingers. 'Ah, well,' is what I say, or sometimes, 'whatever turns you on,' but what I am saying now is that Prof. Weiss, as he began to leaf through the book, gave a wonderful imitation of a cleanly smoker who has borrowed a box of matches from one of the above.

'Hmmm,' he hmmmed, after conning a few of the early interleaves, '*hmmm*. Evidently some diligent but unpromising young Grecian wrote these *postilla*, the sort of boy who used to come here to Scone because he was afraid of Balliol. I've seen hundreds of them, hundreds; at the end of their first term I usually advise them to change over to one of these new, bogus disciplines. English Literature or Sociology or something of that sort.' He closed the book with a snap.

'Well, good day to you, Mr er ah um; won't you have a little more wine? No? Must you go? Can't you stay? Such a shame; I was enjoying our little chat.'

Look, I really do have the greatest respect for my elders and academic betters; *reverentia* is meat and drink to me. On the other hand, I had eaten quite enough shit for one afternoon, especially since I was committed to dining at High Table later on.

'Professor Weiss,' I said, gently but crisply, 'if you will be good enough to lift the domestic telephone which I see beside your right elbow and ask the Lodge to connect you with the Warden, he will assure you that I have not called to waste your time discussing the second-hand book market but to enlist your help in a matter of grave concern to the College. Or perhaps you will take my word for this? You will? Good. Then pray be so kind as to cast your eye over the manuscript passage which begins where I have inserted a large, readily-visible book-marker which I am sure you cannot have failed to notice. What I need is a quick construe. *Graecum est, non legitur*, you see.'

He blinked, rose to his feet and unerringly found a bottle of San Patricio Fino and filled two rare and beautiful glasses. Then he put on some stronger spectacles and began to scan the ball-pointed interleaves.

'τάδε γράφω περὶ τοῦ βίου μου φοβούμενος,' he began lucidly. '"*I write this in fear of my life*" is what is meant I imagine, but βίος is quite the wrong word, don't you know, it means life as in biography; now ζώης would be all right, as in zoology. What comes next? ἀνιστορῶν γαρ ὅπου οὐχ ἔχρην – "*making enquiries where I should not*" – ἄγαν φανερὸς γέγονα – "*I have become too conspicuous*" – well, yes, that's clear enough but not very elegantly put – τῷ 77844 προσέχων τὸν νοῦν – "*while applying myself to 77844*" – though I must say I don't

care for that asyndeton – ἔξ απροσδοκήτου
μεμάθηκα – "I have unexpectedly learnt" – πῶς ἄρα ἐ
φονεύθησαν οἱ ἐν 548923, καὶ ἄνθρωπον
εὕρηκα περισωθέντα – "how the people at 548923
were massacred; and I have found a survivor."'

He sucked in a mouthful of sherry, patted dry his wine-
soaked moustache, drew a gurgle from his egregious pipe,
cleared his throat and made, with some reluctance, as
though to continue. One might have thought he was
playing for time; it certainly gave me time to think: pennies
dropped, bells rang and sirens screamed in my craven brain-
pan. I leapt to my feet and snatched the dangerous vol.
from his hands as courteously as one can snatch vols from
the hands of Professors of Greek Palaeography; nor did I
stand upon the order of my going.

'Thanks awfully,' I gibbered, 'sorry to waste your time,
do forgive me, clearly someone earning a little pin-money
writing trashy thrillers, wouldn't you say? Eh? Delicious
sherry, how kind, silly of me, shouldn't have taken up your
valuable wine – time, I mean – most kind ...'

He peered at me thoughtfully through spectacle-lenses
as thick and obscure as boiled sweets. As I eyed the eyes
behind them, which floated like dead goldfish in bowls, I
remembered that I had forgotten that he had to be a great
deal brainier than me.

'No,' he said, 'it is you who are kind. I should very much
have disliked to read any more of this "thriller," as you are
pleased to call it. Certain ah, extra-mural work I did during
the War impressed on me vividly that one's expectation of
life is greatly increased by suppressing any curiosity about
matters outside one's own field. The heroine of your thriller
seems to have learned this lesson too late, wouldn't you
say?' I mumbled something as I edged towards the door.

'Splendid. Splendid. Good afternoon, Mr er ah um ...'

I opened my mouth to say 'Mortdecai' but he was faster
on the draw.

'The Hon. Charlie Strafford van Cleef Mortdecai,' he
mumbled sleepily. 'Came up in '50, did you not; scraped
through Prelims, spent your second year drinking and

wenching, pulled yourself together in your third and managed a respectable Second Class Honours. I ran across one of your contemporaries the other day: Cadbury. He was *clever*.' He pronounced the word as though he rarely used it. 'Good afternoon again, Mr er ah um.'

I tottered out into the bitter-lemon-coloured sunshine, feeling some three inches shorter. My feet were cold; the book in my hand was furnace-hot. It had taken a dotard to teach me just how hot. The Quadrangle was busy with men who might have been undergraduates, girls who might have been boys, people who might have been anything – who can tell nowadays? I ducked back into Professor Weiss's staircase (no. XXXIX if you want to know), tucked the incandescent vol. under my waistcoat, counted to one hundred and sauntered forth again, my hands empty, my back stooped, my face contorted with scholarly thought, like a visiting American Professor giving his celebrated impersonation of a visiting American Professor. I was uncomfortably aware of the fact that my anguished nerve-endings were fiercely protruding from every pore and follicle.

I sank into Bronwen's armchair and coaxed them back inside by inhaling Scotch whisky like a distraught suction-pump. I shut my eyes and turned them on my heart, a tip I got from Childe Roland. It is a well-known medical fact that any Scotch, taken internally, will retract protruding nerve-endings, but only a few specialists are aware that very *good* Scotch, such as I was administering, is rich in all kinds of rare minerals, congeners and esters; it acts directly on the grey brain-cells, stirring the idle little blighters into frenzied activity. Ever so slowly I became aware of a prickling, formicating kind of sensation inside my skull as synapse after synapse thronged around and in a few minutes I opened the eyes, snapped the fingers and said, 'Tom Cadbury! The very chap!' I seized the house-telephone, buzzed the Lodge.

'Fred,' I said, 'where is Mr Cadbury?'

'Still at All Souls, far as I know, sir.'

'Try and get him for me, please.'

Ten minutes later I had trousered the *Lexicon*, along with a pair of Bronwen's scissors, and was swooping, gowned, towards All Souls. En route, I stopped off at Queen's where, anonymous in my gown, I cunningly purchased two packets of envelopes emblazoned with the Queen's College coat of arms. These, too, I pocketed.

I left Queen's and swiftly made my way to the nearest newsagent to have a bash at one of those new-fangled "Xerox" machines. Photocopies carefully concealed in my innermost breast pocket, I set off to find my old mate, Tom Cadbury.

In the appointed room at All Souls I found a pale-pink, portly, bald chap – amazing how some people age in twenty years or so, isn't it?

'Hullo, Charlie,' he said cheerily, then: 'Good God, what *have* you done to your face?'

XIII

Dealer's choice: seven-card stud. Again.

Alas! I tread an endless maze
That seeketh to accord two contraries.

'What cheer, young Thomas,' I rejoined with equal cheeriness, then: 'Good God, what *have* you done to your pate? Why the disaster area, the barren plain, the stricken field?'

'Work and care, old top; care and work.'

'Precisely what I apply to the upper lip – and with rather more pleasing effect. But more to the point, what are you *doing* here? I mean, last time I saw you, a mere twenty years ago, you had just penned a stiff letter to the Dean of All Souls, curtly refusing their offer of a Fellowship in no ambiguous terms. I posted the letter for you as I left, if memory does not fail me.'

'Ah, yes, well, it was all rather strange, almost surreal. You see ...'

But it occurs to me that the ensuing dialogue will prove incomprehensible to any reader not steeped in All Souls lore, unless I weigh in with a brief prologue.

All Souls, you must understand, is an odd College, even

by Oxford standards of oddness. It was founded five centuries ago by one H. Chichele, who'd made a good thing out of being Archbishop, and it is a fine example of 'all chiefs and no Injuns': just a Warden, forty Fellows and four 'Bible Clerks' – all of whom had to be kinsmen of the said Archbp., which must have made its first lot of dons something of a mixed bag, for Chichele sprang from what is politely called 'yeoman stock.' Their only duty, originally, was to pray for the souls of those killed in Henry V's French Wars and to be *'bene nati, bene vestiti et modice docti'* – 'well bred, well dressed and moderately well educated.' Of course, All Souls has changed with the times a bit, nowadays likely contenders for Fellowships have to be very well *docti* indeed and skilled in the art of eating cherry pie. Prospective F.'s are asked to dine, you see, and on such occasions the sixth or seventh course is always cherry pie. There is only one way of disposing of the cherry pits which is acceptable at All Souls and it's a closely-guarded secret. Spitting them over your shoulder, for instance, is practical but not considered *bene natus.* Now read on.

'You see ...' Thomas Cadbury was saying, 'that letter of refusal you so officiously posted for me was really more of a displacement activity than an actual refusal because no-one had offered me any such Fellowship. I'd spent the previous evening with you, if you recall, and had naturally woken up with the sort of hangover which makes you want either to disembowel someone or to write a stiff letter. Since you had not yet appeared that a.m. I had to fall back on the stiff-letter ploy and I must say I felt the better for it until later, when I realised you'd actually posted the blasted thing. Judge of my amazement when, by return of post, I received a letter from the muddle-headed old codger who was Dean here in those days, infinitely regretting my refusal and asking me to show that there were no hard feelings and come and have a bite with him on the following Thursday week. I jolly nearly wrote back to say that I didn't expect to be hungry on the following Thursday week but that would have been a falsehood, because in those days I was invariably peckish of a Thursday. So I turned up, as *bene vestitus* as a borrowed dinner-jacket could make me, and had a grand time, browsing and sluicing quite as freely as the phalanx of Fellows around me. Indeed, I recall telling a learned genealogist opposite me that the ninety-third in succession to the Throne was a chap called Browne-Windsor. Then something quite dreadful happened: a plate was slid in front of me groaning under a dashed great slab of pastry laden to the plimsoll-line with cherries!'

'My dear chap,' I said, aghast. 'Tell me, what did you do with the stones?'

'Well, the sight of the confection sobered me up more than a little, but not enough to make a snap judgement in a matter of that gravity so, pending a decision, I sort of tucked them in my cheeks until I must have looked like an unusually provident chipmunk. Then I felt a sneeze coming on and, well, not to put too fine a point on it, Charlie, I swallowed the bloody things.'

'My word, Tom,' I said admiringly, 'I'd never have thought you had it in you!'

'You'd have thought so if you'd passed me in the street on my way back; I must have been rattling like a Salvation Army collection-box. But come, I am neglecting you, dear old friend of my youth. Do you still take a little brandy at this time of the afternoon? I'm sure you do, you were ever a steadfast soul. There. Now, I'm sure you aren't here just to feast your eyes on me – what's the trouble? Where does it hurt?'

Instead of answering, I dealt him a poker-faced hand of credentials. First the Warden's letter, then the Duke's and finally, when his eyebrows were already raised to where he had once kept his hairline, my warrant as Detective Inspector. I have never seen a man boggle so vehemently; I began to fear for his health.

'Charlie,' he said at length, 'when last heard of you were an art-dealer; don't attempt to deny it. Why, of a sudden, have you gone over to the right side of the law?'

'Look, I honestly can't tell you now – perhaps ever. In any case, if what I suspect is as nasty as I fear, you are far better knowing nothing about it. What I need is some unlikely but simple help from you, combined with as much lack of curiosity as you can muster. Are you on?'

'Well, of course. Ask away.'

'How many reasonably capable young Greek scholars could you lay hands on in, say, a couple of days? Six? Eight?'

'Eight should present no difficulty.'

'Now then, observe: I cut these Xerox copies of Greek manuscript into eight irregular, random-shaped pieces, numbering each and jotting down the position of each piece in this notebook. Now I number each of these larger envelopes and insert a piece in each, along with a smaller envelope, also numbered. I seal the larger envelopes. Now your task is to issue one envelope to each scholar *in private*, telling him some rubbish about a bet you have with someone at Queen's. They are to construe their fragments, saying not a word to anyone. To confuse the issue, you might say that they should guess at the missing parts of any mangled words. They must return their fragments by College messenger, sealed in the smaller envelopes. I appreciate that this all seems a trifle daft but you have my word that it is both necessary and bloody serious. I'll call back in, say, three days. OK, Tom?'

'OK, Charlie,' he said, shaking a glum and puzzled head. It is not everyone who is lucky enough to know a distinguished Grecian who can be relied upon utterly; I felt rich in his friendship. Walking back to College I also felt several stones lighter around the shoulders. Then, suddenly, I felt several tons heavier around the conscience, for I had, after all, left my staunch chum in possession of what might well be a danger to him if, for instance, any pairs of large men had been spying on my movements. I sped back to All Souls Lodge and demanded petulantly why Dr Rowse was not in his rooms when he *knew* I was coming, I'd *written* to him.

'He's in Cornwall, sir,' said the porter. I stamped a petulant foot and minced away. Dirk Bogarde couldn't have done it better.

At Scone Lodge I found Fred struggling into his mackintosh with all the signs of a porter who is going off duty.

'Evening, sir; that horse of yours won 'safternoon.' Hell's foundations seemed to quiver; the natural order of things was standing on its head and wiggling its toes.

'Are you jesting with me, Fred?' I asked severely.

'No, sir. Eleven to two plus the place money, minus the betting-tax, let's see ...'

'Don't tell me, Fred, this has come too late in life for me to cope with at short notice. Put the winnings on some other chunk of pet food for me tomorrow – some creature which cannot conceivably win; I am too stricken in years to change my ways and start winning. But meanwhile' – for I saw the disappointment on the honest fellow's face – 'meanwhile, pray let me buy you a great pot of ale at the White Horse and give you a sound thrashing at shove-ha'penny, what? Eh?' He beamed, for he yields to none in the matter of ale-quaffing, while his prowess at shove-ha'penny is legendary.

The White Horse in the Broad is the Mecca of ha'penny-shovers; I had quite forgotten how fast its Guinness-burnished shove-h. board is, so I had lost three games at one pint per game before I could recapture the smooth, oiled wristiness required. Fate was tittering in its sleeve, though, for just as I prepared to trounce Fred on the fourth game (for in my salad days I had been a formidable shover of such coins) he reminded me that it was a Guest Night at High Table and that I would have to get my skates on if I wished to be suitably dinner-jacketed in time.

You would not wish to read what I could write about that dinner: when you have chewed one dead dog, you have chewed them all. It was a demoralised napkin that I trooped into the Common Room for dessert and, later, a demoralised moustache which quivered at the glass of port I had to expose it to. (There's a great deal to be said in favour of a cup of hemlock, you know; at least you drink it in confidence that you won't have to drink the same on the following night.)

Dryden and I were propped dyspeptically against a sofa in the SCR when old Weiss came pottering up to us.

'Ah, Tutor in Renaissance English Language and Literature,' he said – for that is correct form in the better class of SCR.

'Ah, Tutor in Greek Palaeography,' rejoined Dryden more succinctly, 'do you know Warden's Fellow in Sociology? C. Mortdecai?'

'Delighted, Mr er ah um,' said Weiss, lending me a handful of fingers to shake (thus subtly suggesting that I couldn't possibly be an Oxford man). 'I daresay,' he said vaguely, 'that, with a name such as yours, you will be a keen reader of *Civiltá Cattolica*, will you not? The Jesuit newspaper, you know.'

'I'm afraid not, really. Never mastered Vaticanese; it's all Greek to me, ha ha.' He let that pass, but those dead goldfish floated meaningfully behind the lenses.

'A pity,' he said. 'Wonderful people, the Jesuits. So good at so many things: they can turn their hand to anything – tropical medicine, tergiversation, patristic theology, prevarication, there's no end to their gifts. Someone said to me the other day that *Civiltá Cattolica* combined the profundity of Mr Hugh Hefner with the veracity of the *Völkischer Beobachter*; rather good that, eh? Eh? Daresay you've read their edition of *Acts and Documents of the Holy See Relative to the Second World War*? No? Oh, but you should; it's quite a, ah, *thriller*, you might say. It was published in 1966, as I'm sure you know, and it's fascinating on the subject of Polish diplomatic memoranda to Pius XII about the treatment of the Jews. Quite fascinating.' And with that he drifted away, doubtless to enliven some other group. Dryden seemed mystified:

'Weiss is not noted for his lucidity, nor for any great skill at small talk, but I have never heard him actually *burble* before. Whatever can he have meant?'

'I don't know, John,' I said slowly, 'but I rather think he meant *something*. In fact, he may have been suggesting that it was a pleasant evening for a solitary stroll. You will forgive me, won't you? Perhaps I might call at your rooms for a nightcap later?' I, too, drifted away – and out of the College, dumping my gown at the Lodge and borrowing a decayed waterproof to hide my resplendent dinner-jacket with its little red *bouton* of my *Légion d'honneur* (fifth class). Towards the Black Friars' priory in St Giles is where I slunk – that street which could have been one of the loveliest in Europe if only ... oh, never mind. The Black Friars kennelled behind the forbidding portals of their monkhouse are Dominicans, you understand: '*Domini Canes*' – the Hounds of God. More to the point, they do not actually go out of their way to cuddle up to the Jesuits, their brothers in Christ. I don't know why that is. What I do know is that if you happen to want a frank and open-hearted appraisal of some Jesuit publication you don't pop over and ask the nearest Jesuit, do you? (Most priests are so bad at their jobs. Jesuits are far too good at theirs. I mean, you drop in on one and ask an innocent question about, say, Pausanias of Lydia and he simply tells you the answer, whereas what you were secretly hoping for was a brisk attack on your disbelief. If you are reduced to throwing yourself onto the carpet, kicking your legs and whimpering, he diffidently suggests that you might perhaps try going to church. Any church. He doesn't say come back in a week, he doesn't give you any little booklets or *bondieuseries*; it's the soft sell. My art-dealing father did it beautifully, raising the customer's hackles by suggesting that he was *not quite ready* for a Bernini bust or that the pair of Nollekens were perhaps a little too grand for the customer's collection as it stood. Furriers are good at this, too; when a rich old lady asks the price of a mink the furrier smiles pityingly, as though to suggest that she is shopping above her income. She buys the fur.)

No, if you want an opinion on Jesuit matters, you do not pop over to the nearest Jesuit, you pop over to the nearest Dominican, which is precisely where I was popping. The lay-brother who squinted at me through the grille didn't at all like the look of me until I opened my mackintosh and gave him a flash of my dinner-jacket, saying that I was an old pupil of Brother Lucas. Then he *really* hated me, for dinner-jackets are Worldly, you see, and Br Lucas is a world-wide authority on medieval heraldry, revered by one and all, and a notorious pain in the arse. The lay-brother admitted that Vespers were over and I made my way to Br Lucas's cell, which was pretty cosy as cells go. He didn't have to call me 'Mr er ah um;' Bros call you 'my son' if they can't remember your name.

'Fr,' I said courteously (for you don't call them 'Br' unless you're a Br yourself), 'I derived so much pleasure and profit from your seminar on the Heraldry of Augmentations in er ah um that I feel emboldened to draw upon your learning in two slight matters.'

'Go on, my son,' he murmured, ignoring the bottle of vodka which had slipped from my pocket onto his prie-dieu. (Well they are a mendicant order, aren't they; they're forbidden to indulge in stinking pride.) I said that my first problem concerned the 'tierced in pairle reversed' of the von Haldermanstettens: a famous heraldic crux which I hoped would give him a happy ten minutes of pedantry. He dried up after six minutes so I tickled him up by asking wilily why *or* and *argent* were juxtaposed in those arms, contrary to all the laws of blazonry. He revived, expounded lavishly. I snoozed with my eyes open. So can snakes. Then I hit him with the other question.

'I was thinking,' I said coyly, 'of writing a little piece for a popular magazine about the difficult task H.H. Pope Pius XII had when it looked as though the Axis powers were certain to win World War II.' His eyelids drooped sleepily. When a Dominican's eyes droop sleepily it means that the Dominican is very wide awake indeed; even I know that.

'To be frank, Fr,' I went on awkwardly, 'the sort of fee I'm offered by the magazine does not warrant my doing a lot of research, you understand, and I'm told that, in fact, all the relevant documents were published in 1966.' He made a fat, happy noise, like a Pursuivant on a bend sinister.

'Edited by the Jesuits?' I murmured delicately.

' "Edited" is an excellent word,' he murmured back. I cleared my throat.

'Would you advise me to study this collection? In particular, would I find in it all the Polish diplomatic memoranda to the Vatican concerning, well, for instance, liquidation of Jews?' He seemed to have fallen asleep. When Dominicans seem to have fallen asleep, even the hardiest Jesuit climbs the nearest tree and pulls it up after him. I waited, my hands folded in my lap to conceal the fact that I had crossed a pair of fingers.

'Tell me,' he murmured drowsily, 'what does Flavius Josephus, that meticulous gossip-writer, tell us about Our Saviour?'

'Why, nothing,' I said. 'It is a puzzling omission.' He nodded.

'And what does the New Testament tell us about Our Saviour's life from puberty until His early thirties?'

'Nothing,' I said again, puzzledly.

'And what, in the Sherlock Holmes story of *Silver Blaze*, was the significance of the dog that barked in the night?'

'The fact that the dog did *not* bark, Fr,' I said patiently. 'But now, touching on this matter of the 1966 *Acts and Documents* ... oh, yes, sorry, your point is taken. The old *argumentum a silentio*, what? Oh dear. Quite. Yes. Well, thanks awfully, Fr. Goodnight.'

He waved a benign brace of fingers at me and was piously approaching the prie-dieu before I was out of the door.

--- · --- · --- · ---

Furiously was how I mused on my way back across the Quadrangle to the late Bronwen's set. This musing may not have been what P.G. Wodehouse would have described as 'all to the gravy' but it was just gravid enough to give me sufficient sense to call at the Porter's Lodge, stuff the *Shorter Greek Lexicon* into an envelope addressed to one Col. Blucher at the US Embassy, London, and tell Fred to post it in two days unless I collected it beforehand – *in person* and unaccompanied. I asked him to repeat these instructions and, when he had them word-perfect, I released the captive pound note which flirted coyly between my thumb and forefinger.

How strange are the workings of Providence, to be sure! As I mounted the staircase to Bronwen's rooms, not a single electric lightbulb was in action – but then, they never are in the better class of College, are they?

Nonetheless, there was something not actually wrong, but sort of not quite right; I could feel it in me water, as Jock would say. I am zonk-prone, you see: people are forever zonking me with blunt instruments, sometimes on the base of the skull, sometimes behind the ear; they never tire of it, I know not why.

Look, I think it is only fair that I should set out for the innocent reader the limits and parameters of my idiocy and cowardice, those two heaven-sent gifts which help a chap survive into what I choose to call early middle age. Reader, are you over the age of eight? Good. Then you must at some time have found yourself embroiled in some frightful catastrophe, such as an outbreak of fire in a theatre. Being the shrewd and sturdy chap that you must be (having pursued my simple narrative so far), you will have observed that in such an imbroglio three distinct kinds of idiot can be seen by the naked eye.

First; the staunch, officer-type idiot (usually sporting one of those absurd little moustaches which – unlike some I could name – are scarcely worth the mulching) who leaps onto a seat and in staunch, officer-type tones, commands everyone to keep calm, stay in their seats and on no account to panic.

Second; the idiots who listen to him, keep calm, stay in their seats and get incinerated.

Third; the idiots who, seeing no survival value in keeping calm and not panicking, rush to the exit and get trampled to death. Unless they happen to be among the leaders at the exit.

I am happy to say that I belong to this third class of idiot and, being pretty fleet of foot for my age, have always contrived to be placed amongst the first three out of the exit. I'm not saying that this is altogether creditable, nor that my mummy would have approved, but I am alive, am I not? Perhaps this is a good thing. I'm sure my life insurance company thinks so although again, my mummy might raise an objection, not to mention an eyebrow.

What I'm leading up to in my diffident sort of way is that when the Mortdecai second sense – no, I don't mean sixth sense, I was never a braggart – when, I say, the M. second sense tells me that large, rough men are about to bonk me on my valuable skull, I tend prudently to trip away in an opposite direction and a rapid, silent fashion.

So Mortdecai, the portly survivor, marched briskly past the oak – that's Oxford for outer door – of Bronwen's rooms and *audibly* began to turn the next turn and mount the next flight of the staircase. How clever I was, to be sure. The flat of an overdeveloped foot met my chest firmly and in no time I was on my back, precisely at Bronwen's oak. Someone of great strength raised me courteously to my feet, supported my neck with the inside of his elbow and barked the word 'Shoddop!' in my left ear. With a delicate tact of which Jock himself would be proud, he persuaded me to hand over my keys.

XIV

Dead man's hand

Wherewithall, unto the heart's forest he flies,
Leaving his enterprise with pain and cry;
And there he hides, and does not appear.

I need hardly say that I was not quite so deeply slumberous
as I chose to pretend, but contrived to lie doggo while my
assailants, who were two in number, rummaged or 'frisked'
my person. This rummaging or frisking was superficial, you
might say, rather than *intimate*; the rummagers were
evidently looking for something too large to be tucked away
in some nook or cranny of my personal plumbing. Something
readily found: a pistol, perhaps, or – God forbid – a book.

They slid my better wallet (sealskin) out of the inside
breast pocket of my costly raiment but I was drowsily
confident that they would find nothing in it except for a
business card or two, an old photograph of Ingrid Bergman,
an out-of-date Diner's Club card and the £10 which we all
carry these days, don't we, so that the muggers can dash off
to 'make a connection' and get their fix without wasting
precious time kicking you to death. One likes these little
transactions to be carried out with a maximum of civility
and a minimum of blood or faeces, eh?

If these assailants had been cleverer they would have awakened me and asked where the other wallet was – even a CIA man would have known that there had to be another. Or at least they could have lent a little colour to their assault by nicking the tenner – I mean, you and I would have, wouldn't we? But no; when I came to my full senses I found the contents of the wallet intact. Which is more than I can say for Bronwen's set.

— - — - — - — - —

Even Jock would have been alarmed – having failed to derive any satisfaction from my person, as it were, my new friends appeared to have uprooted Bronwen's African violets, smashed to smithereens her wireless and ransacked her record collection – a suprisingly jazzy assortment for a hag such as Bronwen (but one never can tell with these baggy-clothed, saggy-boobed academic women, a fact I once had the unexpected pleasure of discovering in the stacks of the Bodleian a fair few years ago). Most alarmingly, the rooms were strewn with my quality bespoke suitings. Framed prints, all rather predictably Ashmolean and Tate Gallery posters of the Pre-Raphaelites, had been hoisted off walls and tossed on the floor. Only Bronwen's books were of any potential value and then only to an antiquarian bookseller or bibliophile. Most of them were now radically abridged, if you know what I mean: they had been flung across the study with great zeal and some clever cretin/inbred must have taken a surprisingly long time to ascertain that ripping up books was not a particularly effective method of finding whatever it might be that they were hoping to find.

The only thing they had left undisturbed was that damned nuisance of a pink piggy-wig. I suppose even the Shoddopsky twins had their limits.

As I surveyed the wreckage of a once orderly, if rather dull, set, I felt my head begin to spin far more dramatically than after I'd imbibed several bowls of Armagnac chased down with a late-night bucket's worth of inferior whisky. And knowing that I could not secure one of Jock's famed emergency kits, I began to feel the floor slipping away again as I lurched rather inelegantly onto the rummaged bedclothes that littered the lumpy bed.

When I next woke, it was a rather bitter and mournful Mortdecai who found that he had just spent an uncomfortable night curled up next to that odious pig-thing. The Mortdecai brain-pan still reeled and throbbed and there was little I could do to relieve it but sedate myself with aspirin and regular medicinal shots of whisky. I decided (or rather, my health decided for me) that it was best not to go out at all that day.

Turner, uncharacteristically shocked by the state of the rooms and the uncharacteristically large tip I proffered, set to work repairing the damage and restoring order in a fashion not dissimilar to that Mrs Spon might have employed – perhaps I'd underestimated the scout's abilities after all. It was he, note, who brought me hot food in covered dishes from the college dining room and even managed to find some remotely palatable steak and kidney pie with mashed potatoes, a bottle of passable Claret, a large chunk of exceptionally well matured Cheddar and some quite decent port, though I can't imagine where – or how – in such a place as Scone he might have come by it.

The following morning I was relieved to find that the pain in my skull had abated almost completely. I made an uncharacteristically early sortie to the Buttery and returned to my rooms with intent to plan the day before me. It cannot have been long afterwards that the tinkle of the phone roused me from what I must confess was something of a zizz.

'Charlie?' It was Tom.

'Tom,' I said, choosing my words carefully.

'Something of a problem, old chap, I'm afraid.'

'Concerning, ah, your students' *assignments?*' I enquired elaborately, raising a telephonic eyebrow.

Tom paused for an instant, clearly a little confused; there followed the inaudible sound of a penny dropping before he continued: 'Indeed, yes. Seven of them have, er, got full marks, I'm pleased to report, but one of them, er, hasn't done his essay at all. I popped round to his rooms, and no-one's seen him since we had our last, um, tutorial. Most odd – he was something of a star pupil, you understand. Chap by the name of Stephanovich.'

The dots in my head began to connect and I said hurriedly. 'I think we'd better discuss this in person – are you in for the next half-hour or so?'

'Yes, of course. I say, Charlie, you wouldn't care to—'

'Smashing. I'll be round shortly.' I replaced the receiver with a distinct thunk.

I didn't go round to All Souls immediately, however. There was – need I say? – a question which I had to put to Professor Weiss. An urgent question. I donned my gown – for it was raining a little – and scurried across the Quad in a dignified way, like a don pursued by a female reporter.

You probably know that a set of rooms at Oxford has two outer doors. The inner outer door is a sort of door, so to say, used merely as a door; you know, it's useful to have something to open and shut as you go in and out. The outer outer door is called an 'oak' and it's much more important: if you close it you are said to have 'sported your oak' and that means you are studying away at Greek epigraphy or a Cypriot lift-boy and must not be disturbed for anything less than an atom bomb on Cambridge.

Professor Weiss's oak was not sported. Because he was senior to me I rapped at his inner outer door and counted to ten before opening it.

His lovely antique Persian carpet was in a disgraceful state: they're never the same after being drenched with a couple of gallons of blood, ask any good dry-cleaner. Prof. Weiss looked more senior to me than when I'd last seen him; professors are never the same in such circumstances either.

I am a slave to most of the vices but even my mother would not have accused me of understatement, so I shall not say that his throat had been cut. I mean, a throat sort of starts at the front collar-stud and only goes back an inch or so, wouldn't you say? On the other hand, it would be extravagant to say that his head had been cut off, because there was quite a bit of gristle and so forth holding it on to the rest of him. I didn't feel his pulse; even a policeman would have guessed that the poor gentleman hadn't cut himself while shaving.

'DON'T TOUCH ANYTHING' was what I remembered from the trashy thrillers I read in my youth, so I only threw a couple of books into the blood and used them as stepping stones while I searched Prof. Weiss's pockets. The contents of his wallet were of no interest: reader's cards to some obscure, scholarly libraries, the photograph of an aunt-like person and enough money to buy luncheon at a Greek restaurant. One of his keys opened a steel filing cabinet, which looked more promising. I found his daybook in the top drawer; it contained an entry which read: 'C. Mortdecai called; insolent pup; prying into B.F.'s death; shewed me *regrettable* manuscript of hers. People should leave such things alone.'

———————

Like many a practised coward, whenever I find that I have lifted something too heavy – or too hot – I tend to squeal for help. I'm that sort of a chap. On this occasion I resorted to Jesus.

Jesus College is one of those frightful places in Turl Street, Oxford (England) and is a sort of enclave of the Principality of Wales – indeed, it is said that if you stand in the Quadrangle of Jesus and bellow 'MR JONES!' fifty grimy windows will open and fifty melodious voices will reply, 'Yes, boyo?'

I did not bellow, for my friend there is a Fellow of that College. (He was once a Balliol man but has fallen upon evil times, you understand.) In any case, his name is not Jones but something else which I cannot spell. He was in his rooms. I said that I needed to use his telephone *importantly* and he twigged in a second, being Welsh, you see – devious, *devious*. He made a tactful exit, saying only that he hoped I would join him for a beer in the Common Room when I had finished. I shuddered, for the beer in Jesus College (Oxford) is very nearly as foul as in Jesus College (Cambridge). Never trust a race which has not invented a national drink of its own, take my word for it. (I refer to the Welsh, of course, but you may apply it to Cambridge men if you care to.)

The American Embassy was still at 24 Grosvenor Square (although the Arabs probably own the freehold now) and the telephone number was still as I remembered it and one was still clicked and tinkled through the PXs from one furry-voiced secretary to another until one was privileged to speak to the highest-paid, most wild-mink-voiced one of all. I remembered her from a few years back; well, at least I remembered her fantastic tits, the ultimate status symbol for secretary owners. She remembered me all right, too, but I wasn't going to get any mileage out of that, for she was one of those rare people who do not like me. She made me spell my name three times, then looked me straight in the eye – yes, down the *telephone* – and assured me that there was no such person as Colonel Blucher and yes, she was his Confidential PA but she had never heard of him and gosh she was sorry but there was a call coming through on the hotline from Afghanistan and goodbyeeee. I said something to her which no gentleman should have known how to pronounce. She said, 'You're very welcome,' and we both put our instruments down. Telephones, you understand.

I did not seethe, nor did I fume, for my highly-qualified physician has promised me that seething and fuming are almost as harmful as cigarettes. I rummaged my Welsh friend's set of rooms for something to appease my screaming stomach but there was nothing, nothing; not even a leek. Even I could not bring myself to make a bad joke about that.

Furiously, I span the telephone dial and after only three mistakes I was connected to my wife in Jersey, if you see what I mean. She seemed to think, at first, that I was the taxi-driver, for she was about to travel to the airport, where she intended to climb aboard an aircraft.

'Yes, dear?' she said when I had established my identity. I held the telephone a little further from my ear because icicles were stabbing out of it.

'Listen, Johanna,' I snarled.

'I am doing so, dear; and, so I guess, are most of the servants. You are interfering with their television. But do go on.'

'Johanna dearest, light of my life, apple of my eye, my first and only love,' I said in carefully-modulated tones, trying not to grate my teeth too loudly, 'it is important to me to get in touch with your brother – you know, Colonel Blucher? My brother-in-law? – *immediately.* His secretary-bird has never heard of him.'

'I know, Charlie dear. She just called me. What she said was, you should just follow the old procedure that you and he used way back when for, uh, when you got kind of scared – you know?'

'I know,' I grated. 'And thanks. Have a nice day.' We hung up almost simultaneously: she was a little faster than the Embassy secretary. A matter of bust-measurements, I suppose – not so far to reach, you see.

Perhaps I should explain at this point that why I so freely splashed words about like 'brother' and 'brother-in-law' was because Colonel Blucher was – indeed, probably still is – Johanna's brother and she is my wife and has papers to prove it, so he is, quite clearly, my brother-in-law, wouldn't you say?

I made a great effort of will and ceased the tooth-grating (for I am no longer a young man) and summoned up the old 'procedure' from some nasty mental cubby-hole. I dialled the number, let it ring the prescribed twelve times, hung up and dialled again. A prescribed, twelve-times rung, hung-up and dialled voice said that yes it *was* the Home & Colonial Stores – what hateful memories this boy-scout-spy nonsense conjured up – and I said that I was Willie and wanted to speak to Daddy because Mom was poorly. I added the word '*ugh*' although it was not part of the 'procedure.' Blucher kept me waiting just long enough to make me feel unwanted but not long enough to allow any hostile wire-tappers or buggers to trace the call. He made affable noises. I tried not to snarl.

'Look,' I said levelly.

'I'm looking, Willie. In fact I can see you clearly.'

'Oh Christ, Franz, if there's one thing more tiresome than a humourless man, it's a humourless man who feels obliged to make funnies. Don't, I beg you. Just listen. A certain lady has recently been treated with what your awful American clandestine people would call "extreme prejudice." Got it?'

He made gotting-it noises of the non-committal sort. I continued. 'She made some cryptic sort of notes before, ah, *leaving*. Got it? Yes, well, people are now creeping up behind me and hitting me cruelly upon what I still like to think of as my head.'

He made standard textbook noises of the sympathetic sort.

'The notes were about a lot of people who were massacred some years ago in a country famous for its chamber-pots – oh dear, sharpen your wits, do: in England the chamber-pot is known to its friends as a "po." *PO* – got it?'

He made baffled noises in his brain – I could hear them – then he got it. 'Yeah, got it. So what else is new?'

'What else is new is disturbing: it seems that my certain lady stumbled across some information which says that the dreadful people who were supposed to have done the massacre didn't; and that it was a different lot. A very different lot indeed.'

'Look, Willie, maybe you know what you're talking about but it's Greek to me.'

I cringed. 'No no *no*, not Greek at all, far from it, rotten shot. It's more, um, Coptic Ethiopian.' (A stroke of inspiration there, for one of the few people I truly hate is the Fellow and Tutor in Coptic Ethiopian. If the line was being bugged by baddies, there was a good chance that the said baddies would give the said Fellow a bad time.)

'Hey, Willie, don't you think you should take an aspirin and kind of sleep a couple of hours? You sound a little confused, sort of tired and emotional, you know?'

The Mortdecai teeth began to grate again, although I had bidden them not to.

'Franz,' I grated civilly. 'I am not drunk. I am never drunk at this time of day. Are you taping this conversation? You are? Good. Play it back as soon as I have replaced the receiver. Study it. *Think.* I might capture your full attention if I said that the massacre in question took place in 194–

and at a place called, oh, yes, well, let's say its name begins
with the letter—'

'Shut up!' he barked suddenly. I sighed with relief. He
had, at last, really got it.

'Charlie,' he said, his voice switching octaves as he
spoke the one word.

'You mean Willie,' I said.

'Yeah. So enjoy; I made a mistake. Willie, get your ass
over here now. Like *now*.'

'Don't be absurd, Franz; do you realise where I am?'

'Yes, I realise. Just get here.'

'But however could I get to the station … the taxis here! …
and have you *been* on a British Rail train lately? I mean, even if
there were a buffet car, it would be quite … oh, really …'

'OK, OK, you've made your point. Is there anywhere in
your College where a helicopter could land?'

'Well, we do have a sort of lawn in the Quadrangle –
that's like a campus, hunh? – but the helicopter-driver would
be instantly hacked to dolly-rags by enraged Head Gardeners
wielding rakes and I would be stripped of my Honours
Degree, which would be horrid in this inclement weather for
I was always prone to chest-colds, even as a child …'

He said a word which he had doubtless picked up in the
West Point Military Academy for Young Gentlemen; I
riposted with a word I had learnt in the Hailsham College
for the Sons of Officers and Clergymen. Our teeth ground
to a halt; we started afresh.

'OK, Willie,' he started afresh. 'I'll send a car. Be at the
janitor's shack of your school—'

'Porter's Lodge of my College?'

'At the Porter's Lodge of your College in precisely
one hour.'

'Nonsense; it can't be done in the time. Say ninety
minutes.'

'Yes it can. I'm saying sixty minutes. Got it?'

'Yeah,' I said.

To my intense annoyance, a motorcar or automobile
swept up to the gates of Scone College precisely sixty
minutes later. It was some kind of Ford which looked as

though it had served in Northern Ireland; it bore *corps diplomatique* decals and the driver seemed unusually fresh-faced. He didn't get out, he just wound down the window and favoured me with a display of big white teeth which you could construe as a civil smile or dumb insolence, according to how your liver felt that morning.

'Your boss,' I whispered murderously, 'is clearly in a frolicsome mood. To send for me in a grotty old Ford – when he knows that I'm a car snob – oh, *really*!'

His smile or grin stretched wider. I eyed him narrowly. There was a twinkle of chess-playing merriment in his eye which both warned and warmed me. He leapt out with surprising alacrity and opened the door, favouring me with a flourishing bow of which an émigré French dancing-master would have been proud.

I swept into the passenger seat beside him, threw my hastily-packed overnight-bag onto the back seat, and elevated my Graeco-Roman nose in a haughty way. He trickled us through the Oxford traffic in that easy, off-hand fashion which reminds one of Dean Martin singing – he was good, really good. Nevertheless, as we floated up Headington Hill a puzzlement was nagging at me. I cleared my throat.

'Look here,' I said. 'What's your name, eh?'

'Samuel Johnson Brown, Lieutenant, US Army.'

The puzzlement continued to nag. As we approached the roundabout which gives you access to the swings of the motorway – after you've been circling it three times while more seasoned roundabout-users shake their puny fists at you – I cleared my throat again.

'Lt,' I said (and I took great pleasure in pronouncing it in the British manner), 'where did you set out from? I cannot find it in my heart to believe that you did Grosvenor Square to Scone College, Oxford (England) in sixty statutory minutes and in this old heap of battered tin. Pray explain.'

'You heard of manufacturers' specifications? You did? Yeah, well this jalopy didn't. Lie back; enjoy.' Whereby he trod savagely upon the accelerator pedal. I trod savagely on the passenger-brake as my spine hit the cushion behind me.

XV

Ignorant end of the straight

A nere example unto you of my foly and unthriftnes that hath, as I well deseruid, brought me into a thousand dangers and hazardes, enmyties, hatrids, prisonments, despits and indignations.   —*Sir Thomas Wyatt*

B y the time I arrived in Blucher's office – having laboured through the absurdities of US Embassy security – his mood had changed considerably.

'Hello, Charlie,' he said sombrely. He unlocked a drawer in his desk and lifted out Bronwen's *Shorter Greek Lexicon*, which he placed silently onto the Moroccan leather blotter.

'Ah, I see that you've received my book-of-the-month recommendation.'

'Cut the crap, Charlie. This little beaut turned up just after you called. Now, since you're here and since your ass is already on the line, you'll be pleased to know that I've just volunteered you for some civic duty.' He drew a large envelope from another drawer in his capacious desk, and continued with an air of mild irritation. 'Which means, I'm afraid, that you're outta here ...'

Blucher fairly stroked the documents as he drew them from the envelope. 'Temporary Accreditation Wallet – should see that you don't come up against any, uh, *bureaucratic hindrances,* so to speak. Your ticket. Flight leaves at 20.00. Traveller's cheques – they're in US dollars, so you'll need to get them changed when you arrive.'

'Splendid.'

'And finally, the name and address of our top Soviet-ologist. Someone will meet you. I won't give you any more details right now, just in case...'

'Naturally.'

'Great! Any questions?' He put all the paperwork back into the envelope and slid it across the desk.

'No,' I lied.

'Excellent – have a great trip, call me when you get back.'

'You're most kind,' I said, gripping the envelope with not a little disdain.

'Oh, and Charlie? One more thing.'

'Yes?'

'What the hell is that thing on your lip?'

—·—·—·—·—·—

Well, there I was, having imbibed the most perfunctory cup of tea for decades, dragging my baggage (no, I mean my *hand luggage*) for what seemed miles along airport walkways – unaided by human hands because the airport busybodies wouldn't allow even my US Embassy vehicle to park for even an *instant*. Jock would have sorted them out, but Lt Brown had no charisma, few and skimpy muscles all in the wrong places, and bloody Blucher had given us no VIP chit. 'All part of the great plan,' I daresay. ('Never trust a brother-in-law,' is what you probably daresay.)

A sweating Mortdecai heaved himself up the staircase-thing which lets you climb into airplanes, ready to be smiled at and cosseted by charmingly insincere air-hostesses. I had forgotten that I was flying Aeroflot. The insincerity was palpable, the charm was a brief and grudging glimpse of stainless-steel dental work and I had to find my own seat. There is something about me that Russians do not like – it cannot be that I perhaps look just the least little bit Jewish; after all, I was only getting *into* their country, not trying to get out. Perhaps it is because I tend to say, in an effort to please, 'Tovarich!' – perhaps that carries Stalinist or, God forbid, Menshevik overtones. The only other Russian words I know are yes, no and something like 'spats yeh bo' (and I can never remember whether that means 'please' or 'thank you'). Perhaps they don't like the cut of my Vigo Street suits. Whatever the case, they don't like me.

Fortune, however, smiled in a tight-lipped kind of way so far as to afford me a row of seats unoccupied by any human bottom but mine own ill-favoured one (Alexander Pope, 1688–1744). The only harassment was that I had to sit, cigarette-less, for some eighty minutes before we were airborne, listening to egg-laying hen noises from the public-address system and the quite riveting cackle from a breeding-pair of young executives behind me.

When I finally disembarked – dishevelled, disgusted and cursing the Wright brothers – I could have kissed the tarmac, if such a custom were allowed in a Russian airport, that is.

I wasn't expecting to see a chauffeur with a hand-stencilled sign reading "MR C. MORTDECAI – TOP SECRET US EMBASSY BUSINESS" but I did wish that Blucher had given me just a smidgen more to go on. After fully five minutes of keeping my disgruntled moustache waiting, I spied a lissom, blonde and – not to put too fine a point on it – rather delicious girl who seemed, or so I imagined, to be heading in my direction.

'Excuse me,' I asked innocently. 'Would you be so kind as to tell me where I might change some American money?'

'Of course,' she breathed breathily. 'Don't worry about the money now. We get a taxi.'

Well, as I've often said, I am an idiot but I'm not actually stupid, am I? I mean, juicy, flavour-of-the-week, ice-blonde Finnish girls may have their little foibles (in fact, you can have my word on that), but their fancies hardly ever run to slightly overweight British chaps in early middle age who haven't shaved for twelve hours and have just explained that they are having difficulty getting enough kopecks to buy a postcard. This is a well-known tendency. However, I succumbed to my incurable faults of curiosity and salaciousness and got into the nearest taxi with her, whereupon we bumped slowly through the streets of Moscow until we arrived at the Metropole Hotel.

The bleak-eyed hag at reception slid the key to my room across her venom-pitted desk and snarled something full of '*zchu*'s and '*zhnak*'s to my Finny denizen. I raised a worried eyebrow but she explained that the hag was only rebuking her for smoking in public. Screwing, it seemed, was OK but the decencies must be observed. Like, say, not dropping toffee-papers in the Moscow Metro.

As soon as we were in my room she divested me with great zeal and many a well-feigned squeak of admiration; then allowed me partially to do the same for her. I had at last identified the accent of her nearly-perfect English: it was East German, oh dear. However, her Finnish disguise was good: all Baltic girls wear heavily-knitted, double-gussetted knickers except in centrally-heated hotels, where they wear none; every chap who has knocked around the Baltic a bit knows that.

The Metropole's central heating is famed.

Just as I was about to work my wicked will on her (indeed, I was already twirling my moustache in a "Sir Jasper" sort of way) she closed my eyelids with a coy fingertip and flitted towards the bathroom and turned on some taps. I opened one eyelid a coy millimetre and was disappointed to see her flitting silently back to where she had coyly piled my clothes, and commencing to rummage them. 'Oh, *really!*' I thought; 'a chap like me surely rates a better class of spy than this ...' But I had wronged her; all she fished out of my gents' natty suiting was a mere felt pen (I never carry proper fountain pens on Aeroflot, I don't trust the pressurisation of their cabins). I was happy that it was a mere felt pen rather than my razor-sharp gold-nosed Parker, because she wrote upon my actual body with it.

'HUSH,' she wrote. 'THIS ROOM IS BUGGED.' Well, I could have told her that. So we sort of held hands and gazed into each other's eyes, so to say, for ten minutes or so – well, let's say twenty-five minutes, for I am no longer a young man, you know – without the least compunction on my part because, infra-red cameras or not, I can think of no-one who would be interested in a blackmail deal concerning me (Johanna would only get the giggles) and I could hardly be breaking any law unless the Soviet consent law starts at the age of thirty. Then she coyly – she was wonderfully good at coyness – asked me whether I had any traveller's cheques.

All the spice of the adventure vanished: this was, after all, no glamorous spy but just another up-market tramp. Ah, but wrong again is what I was. What she suggested was that we should go to the 'American Attached Officers Club' (well, I guessed what she meant) where they took any currency other than roubles and kopecks. She mumbled into the room-telephone, fumbled herself into her clothes (how cold her poor bottom must have been) and told me to meet her in a large black limousine which would be outside the hotel in some nine or ten minutes.

Now, anyone who has followed my earlier craven adventures may perhaps recall that I have a rooted objection to entering large black limousines – things happen to me when I enter such vehicles. However, Russia cannot yet afford a Mafia (well, no, I'm not taking any bets on that) and the only people there who can afford cars at all have these large black limousines called *Zygs* or something like that. So down I tripped, after a prophylactic wash, and popped into a large black limousine whose driver was beckoning me in a comradely fashion.

The door thunked and I turned to splash a grateful kiss on my luscious little Finesse's cheek as she snuggled in the spacious back seat beside me. Alas, she proved now to be a large, sand-papery Russian, approximately three metres long and three metres wide. (You could tell he was Russian because of his suit, you see.)

'Whoops, sorry!' I tittered. 'Got into the wrong car, haven't I?'

'No,' he said, in perfect English. The limousine slushed away from the kerb and whirred into the less lamp-lit bits of Moscow.

A lesser man would have said, 'Oh *shit*, I've got into one of those large black limousines again; when, when, *when* will I ever learn?' But I, being Charlie Mortdecai, said, 'Oh *shit*, I've got into one of those large black limousines again; when, when, *when* will I ever learn?' and then put on my haughtiest expression and said, haughtily, 'You will let me out at once, please.'

My fellow traveller didn't let me out. What he did let out, from the inside breast pocket of his greatcoat, was the most fearsome weapon I have seen since I caught our charlady with the gardener. Yes, gentle reader, it was a "29." (For even gentler readers I should explain that this means a Smith & Wesson .44 Magnum, Model 29 revolver, the pistol with 30% more clout – muzzle-energy – than its nearest competitor. If anyone points such a thing at you, don't waste your time hiding behind a brick wall: a "29" doesn't even notice such flimsies.)

I pretended to be frightened. This was not difficult. Then I summoned up what English blood I could muster and arranged a tremulous sneer onto my face.

'Do you speak English?' said my face.

'Yes,' he said. I had to admit that his command of English was still perfect. If it comes to that, his command of me just then was pretty adequate.

'Then allow me to explain that the monstrous pistol you are waving about is designed solely for shooting presidents on bullet-proof balconies. If you were so foolish as to loose it off at me here and now, you would make a sorry mess both of my brain-pan and of this valuable limousine; moreover, the noise would be such that even the less curious residents of this beautiful city might make entries in their diaries. So, I am not afraid of you in the least.'

He smacked me across the face with the barrel of his valuable, heavy, American-made pistol. At this point I became afraid of him in the least.

'Shoddop,' he said. I fell silent, not out of any spirit of obedience but because I was busy spitting out a loosened tooth. I had a distinct sense of *déjà vu*. I daresay, now I come to think of it, the limousine's carpet had the same feeling.

'You will now be good, yes?'

Well, I suppose that, had I been a 100% true-born Englishman, I'd have said, 'I defy you to do your damnedest, you dastard,' or, even bravelier, 'I should like to telephone the British Consul, please;' but dentistry is so costly nowadays that what I actually said was:

'Yes.'

In a last flicker of defiance I added the word 'comrade.' He didn't hit me again; what he did do was nestle that terrifying pistol between my thighs – *high* up between my thighs – and smile at me. The smile was daunting enough, for most of his teeth were of stainless steel, but the pistol-barrel really *bothered* me. You see, dying from the blast of a .44 Magnum in what you probably like to think of as your brain is but the work of a moment, whereas the same muzzle-velocity released where the said .44's muzzle was nuzzling would, arguably, have caused me acute discomfort and I'm just British enough to dislike screaming in front of foreigners. Moreover, it might well have taken me quite five minutes to die.

I arranged a polite expression onto the side of my face which had not yet been pistol-whipped.

'Talk,' he said.

Well, I talked, of course. You, who are brave, might not have talked so freely so soon but I, who am worldly-wise, knew perfectly well that at just ten minutes' drive away there was a place where Mr Vitaly Fedorchuk and his lads can make the strongest man whimper for his mummy and his teddy bear inside an hour – with not a mark on his skin. Or his memory. So I talked while the talking was good; that is to say, while I was still cunning and fit enough to lie capably. It seemed to me that if I were sufficiently plausible they would not think it worth making an international scandal by giving me the warm bath business in Lubianka or whatever it's called.

Russian words were exchanged and the car drew up beside the road; the comradely driver came and sat in the back seat with us. He gave me a strong brown paper bag to be sick into: they *know* about things like that. Then I told them everything. Yes, every scrap, for I am a coward, as I never tire of admitting; it seems to keep me alive. Well, in my blabbing I did perhaps make a couple of what my underpaid schoolmasters used to call 'deliberate mistakes:' I foolishly said that it was Professor Weiss who had the Greek manuscript (well, I couldn't get my friend Tom Cadbury into trouble, could I?) and, when I related what I said I thought I seemed to remember of the narrative, I fancy I got the various Great Powers mixed up a bit; but who (as the lady said when she offered her guest the fifth Künzl Fancy Cake) is counting?

Curiously, they seemed quite satisfied. Did I want to catch a plane?

'*Spats yeh bo!*' I said, in impeccable Russian. '*Da,*' I added, doubling my vocabulary.

Then would I care to sign this document saying that I had caught my poor face in a revolver? I stared at them. The one who spoke English made English gestures suggesting a revolving door. I looked at the document. It might have been in, well, Greek for all I knew. '*Nyet,*' I said bravely, playing my third card. My accent must have been good, for they understood me perfectly.

This time they did not hurt me much, and soon we agreed that I should write just such a legal waiver in impeccable English. I did so. I must have been a little tired, for my signature, although quite like enough to that on my passport to fool benighted Bolshies who read and write in Kyrillic, would not have fooled my bank manager for an instant. He's been fooled by experts, you see. Often.

My two inquisitors, leaving not a rack behind, did not drop me off at the Metropole but at the airport. I hate to disappoint you, but the truth is that, with the aid of Col. Blucher's impressive documents and even more impressive traveller's cheques, in a few hours I was speeding homewards, with only one black eye and one missing tooth. More to my comfort, the speeding homewards was being done in a British Airways aircraft. As I entered this homeward-bound machine a smiling British stewardess, with one of those false smiles which only the British can do properly, gave me a Russian phrase book – honestly! I thanked her with a straight face for this uncovenanted mercy and asked her whether she, too, had lost her sense of direction in Moscow, for the phrase book might have been more useful in Moscow than in Heathrow. She smiled politely; air-hostesses are used to being asked odd questions by people who have had a few drinks to cover up their terror of flying.

I was decidedly overjoyed to see Lt Brown waiting for me at Heathrow, though how he knew I'd be there, I didn't think to wonder. Neither would I have much cared, had I thought to wonder.

'Grosvenor Square?' he asked.

'Good Lord, no!' I exclaimed. I had no desire to see Blucher, and even less intention of enduring a fruitless debriefing at the hands of another jumped-up spy, even one related by marriage.

'Scone College, Oxford,' I said firmly.

XVI

Red queen busts the flush

She took from me a heart and I a glass from her:
Let us see now, if the one be worth the other.

Governesses, be they never so married, are always called Miss or Mademoiselle, everyone knows that. Conversely, housekeepers of canonical age and cooks who are grand enough to have a kitchen-maid to bully are always called Mrs, however intact be their chaste treasure. Both styles of address, after all, are simply short for Mistress – which lies somewhere between a mister and a mattress. Therefore all men and all sensible women deplore the absurd vocable 'Ms,' a coinage so daft that only a bra-burner could have dreamt it up. As a matter of fact it isn't even a vocable at all in the proper sense of the word, for it cannot be pronounced (except in the Ki-N'Gorongoro dialect, of course, where it is made by a wet fluttering of the lips followed by an even wetter sibilance, and means something quite beastly). These petulant remarks of mine are to the point, as you will presently learn, unless you have just wrapped these pages in your bra and touched a match to them.

'You look a bit shot at, Inspector Mortdecai,' said the DCI when I reported to him at lunch time. 'Been working hard at the case?'

'I have certainly not been idle, DCI. Since arriving in Oxford I have interviewed one Warden of Scone, one Duke or Chief Constable, one Detective Chief Inspector, one Domestic Bursar, two Bank Managers, a Lodge Porter, a Junior Dean, a Dean of Degrees, a Protobibliothecarius, a Professor of Greek Palaeography, a Fellow of All Souls and a Dominican monk or friar. In addition I have made the acquaintance of one lady of East German persuasion, two strong handsome men with a mean line in pistol-whipping, and an assortment of air-hostesses.'

'Crikey,' he said. 'What about the Pope, when are you seeing him?' I looked at him strangely.

'Funny you should say that ... however, what I have to report is that I haven't anything to report. That's to say, I rather think I've got a line on the "Why" but it's probably the aspect that Whitehall is anxious to suppress, so I daresay you'd just as soon I didn't go into that, am I right? As to the "Who" and the "How," I'm completely stymied.'

'Tough titty. When are you going to see the husband?'

'See the what what what?' I gobbled. 'What d'you mean, "husband;" what husband, what?'

'Why, Mrs Fellworthy's husband.'

'But she was *Miss* Fellworthy ...'

'No, sir; she was married and separated. Thought you knew.'

'Redundant, mud-headed old prick!' I snarled bitterly. His face froze into that expression which public servants adopt when abused by members of the public in the absence of witnesses.

'No no no, dear old DCI,' I said hastily, 'not you at all; I was thinking of a Fellow and Tutor of my College who should have told me of this husband at the outset.'

'Probably didn't know,' he said mildly. 'She was one of these illiberalated women or whatever they call themselves – we call them baggy-boobs if you'll pardon the term – and she always went by the style of "Ms." ' I gazed at him reverently: he had *pronounced* it. I couldn't resist showing off.

'Did you spend *much* time in the N'Gorongoro country?' I asked in a knowledgeable sort of voice. 'No, never mind, just a thought, just a thought. More to the point; who, what and where is this spouse, this soul-mate, this husband of Bronwen's, er, bosom?'

'He's by way of being a doctor, sir, lives in leafy Bucks., somewhere round Lacey Green way. Wait, here's his card, I've got it right here.' I studied it. W.W. Fellworthy was no mere MB but an actual MD (Oxon), a Fellow of the Royal College of Physicians and – here I raised a respectful eyebrow – a Fellow of the Royal Society to boot and no less.

'An exceedingly pleasant gentleman,' continued the DCI, 'and most upset about the shocking tragedy. Most grieved. Rushed up to Oxford the moment he read about it in the papers, wanted to make funeral arrangements, make his last farewell to the *corpus delicti*. (We had to put him off that, of course, I mean, we'd had to scrape her out of the wreckage like a pot of strawberry jam, as the old song says, and then we'd done the necropsy and they never look the same after that, do they – are you all right, sir? – so there wasn't any way of brushing her lips with a last, chaste kiss because – you *sure* you're all right, sir?) Well, as I was saying, he wanted to collect her personal effects; she hadn't got much except her library of books, which she'd left to some Women's College, but he just wanted her intimate possessions, handbag, glasses – he specially asked for her glasses – little things like that. Sentimental, you see. I could tell he was still passionately enamoured of her, almost weeping at the thought that never again would he slip the diaphanous, silken undergarments from those quivering mounds ...' His eyes hooded, his voice faltered. Either he nourished some hidden, policemanly vein of the true romance or his vice squad had recently raided a pornographic bookshop. My own eyes, too, were a bit hooded, for it seemed to me that only a Quasimodo could possibly bring himself to prise the hairy, orange Donegal tweed from Bronwen's sagging dugs; but there you are, aren't you? I mean, that's what makes horse-races, isn't it?

There was, however, a bit more to the Mortdecai eye-hooding than mere vulgar curiosity about a copper's library-list. There was a distinct bubbling sensation in the porridge which occupies my brain-pan; something had been said which meant something, you see, but I couldn't quite nail it to the counter. Something about intimate possessions. Fellworthy had wanted them. Sentimental, you see. My mind's eye conjured up Bronwen's room and the little, intimate, sentimental trivia which were still lying about there. Like the hateful, fluffy pink piggy-wig nightie-case and the drawers full of sturdy, sensible knickers. Like the porcelain pussy-cats, silver hair-brush and snapshot-album on her messy dressing-table. Like the Parker pen-set and Florentine leather blotter on her tidy desk. *Desk?* Yes, and like the two pairs of spectacles on her desk.

'These, ah, glasses of Mrs Fellworthy's that her husband seemed so keen on,' I said idly, 'I daresay he was glad to have them? I mean, he shed a sentimental tear or two, eh?'

'No.'

'No?'

'No, well we couldn't find them; everything was a bit squashed up, as I already remarked, and we could only find the case. Quite agitated, he was; asked where the wreck was so he could have a look for himself. I told him the name of the garage but advised him most strenuously not to carry out his intention; the wreckage was copiously, er, stained, you understand, and I begged him not to mar the beautiful memories he cherished of her as a radiant young woman in the bloom of her beauty.'

'Hmmm,' I said, voicing my own memories of the living Bronwen, 'do you think you could be terribly kind and get the garage-proprietor on the phone?'

'Certainly, sir.' *Bzzz-bzzz, Bzzz-bzzz.* 'Hallo, Mr Duffy? Got an officer here from, er, London, making routine checks on that crunch in the High Street, yeah the lady-don ... have a word with him?'

'Hullo, Mr Duffy, shan't keep you a moment, just tying up the loose ends before I countersign the DCI's report' – I winked apologetically at the DCI – 'I understand the husband of the deceased driver talked of calling on you to examine the wreckage in person – did he do so?'

'Yeah. Nasty, miserable bugger he was, too. We told him the wreck had gone off to the crusher that very morning and he made a nasty scene, said I'd no right to demolish his property eckcetra.'

'And had it, in fact, gone?'

'Not acksherly, no; it went the next day, but I wouldn't have let me worst enemy see his wife's car all sticky and that and the flies so thick you couldn't hardly get near it.'

'Well, thanks, Mr Duffy. I'm sure you did the right thing, you've obviously got a kind heart.'

'And he'd have had a sore arse from the end of my boot if he'd gone on ranting and raving at me any longer.'

This picture of Dr Fellworthy by no means agreed with the Inspector's description of him as an 'exceedingly pleasant gentleman.' He might, of course, have been suffering from a delayed reaction which needed venting, or he might be one of those chaps who are civil to senior policemen but a little testy towards garage-proprietors. I myself have been civil to many a copper in my time and have, I grieve to admit, sometimes used language to garage-proprietors which would have raised a few eyebrows in the Cavalry Club itself.

'Nevertheless,' I mused inwardly …

'Nevertheless,' I mused aloud to the DCI, 'Fellworthy does seem to have an almost morbid preoccupation with these visual aids of Bronwen's.'

'Sentimental, see. He treated her to them last year, the last time they ever went on holiday together.'

'You mean they were still seeing each other?'

'Oh, ay. The Channel Islands holiday was probably an attempt at reconciliation, like a second honeymoon; you know, trying to see if the flame of connubial fervour could be rekindled by a touch of the old rumpy-pumpy, see?'

'Yes, I see,' I murmured, giving a reflective twirl to the moustachio. 'And that was the last time he saw her, what?'

'Well, no; it was the last time they were "together" as they say, but he used to pop up to Oxford once a term, take her out to lunch and that. *Nil desperandio* seems to have been his motto. She must have been all woman for him to pursue her so doggedly. Tender and true.'

'Did he happen to mention when he was last in Oxford?'

'Don't think so. No, I'm sure he didn't.'

'Lend me a bright constable for a couple of hours, could you?' Within a minute a bright constable clunked in, his eyes shining with pure intelligence. His name was Holmes, which was tough luck on a Detective Constable, and he was put at my disposal.

'Holmes,' I said kindly, 'you are, I can see, a man of tact. Please tactfully telephone around the hotels and motels and find whether, when and where a Dr W.W. Fellworthy stayed in this fair city during this term. Try the Mitre first, then the Randolph, for he is not short of the readies. If he didn't stay the night he will have lunched with a lady at somewhere pretty up-market. If you have no luck, find out which College he was at, he may have been given a bed by some academic crony. No, wait, save time, don't check each College, ask the Faculty of Medicine; they'll know. Got all that?'

'Yessir. Name of Fellworthy, Dr W.W., Tactful enquiries hotels; ditto luncheon head waiters; ascertain College from Faculty of Medicine; query slept in College.'

'Damn shame,' I said as he clunked out, 'that you didn't find the specs. I feel they might have given us a lead.'

'An old lady did.'

'?'

'Find the specs. In the gutter. Brought them in three days after the tragedy, said she'd just found them in the gutter – lying of course, she'd probably meant to flog them for the gold rims and lost her nerve. I never got round to sending them to the bereaved hubbie but if you're going to call on him – and something tells me you are – you might hand them to him while you're there. Save me some trouble and give you a sort of introduction, see. Also, if he has something on his conscience, it might rattle him a bit, cause him to Make a False Move.' He rummaged in a drawer, slid the specs and case complete with evidence tags across the desk to me.

The case was of olive-green crushed Morocco – real, not Rexine – and the contents were equally expensive-looking, real tortoiseshell and hallmarked gold, huge, circular, saucer-sized lenses as worn by the uppity models in *Tatler* and made of that glass which darkens according to the amount of light present. Mind you, when I say 'lenses' I mean 'lens,' for one of them was just a few shards and flinders of glass still gripped by the remains of its crumpled rim. On a corner of the case the initials B.A.F. were tooled in gold. The maker's name was chastely stamped just inside the lip. Sure enough, it was a Channel Islands product and, to my great delight the stamp read:

JNO. BATES
OPTOMETRIST
ST. OUEN JERSEY

My delight sprang from the fact that

JNO. BATES
OPTOMETRIST

is the courteous and genial ophthalmic optician who crafts my own gig-lamps. (Only for reading, you understand, and as a matter of fact I'm a bit coy about letting on that I need them even for that.) He actually loves his work and I have spent many a happy five minutes at his feet, as it were, drinking in such sippets of elementary optical science as he thinks I might be capable of understanding.

'My word, Inspector, this is a slice of luck. This Mr Bates has copious files and a memory like a computer; if there is a lead to be had from these costly corneal correctors then that lead will be in the Bates retrieval-system, depend upon it!' At that moment the door reverberated under what DC Holmes probably thought of as a discreet knock.

'Any luck, Holmes?'

'Yessir; no great problem. Hadn't stayed at the three decent hotels so I set the rest aside and went for the restaurants. Got it second shot, at the Randolph. Head waiter remembers him well; makes a fuss about the wine every time but tips heavy. Accompanied by a right ... I mean a somewhat plain lady.'

'When was this?'

'Saturday last, sir. Lunch-time.' The DCI and I exchanged pregnant glances. Bronwen had died on the Monday.

'Anything else, Holmes?'

'I had a word with the Head Porter, sir. Dr Fellworthy went and fetched the lady's car from the hotel garage himself, brought it round to the front, said he was sorry he'd been so long and the garage-lads were an idle lot, handed the lady into her car most affectionate, waved her goodbye and went back into the hotel for another brandy. Then he sends the porter for his own car, saying to hurry because he had to be in Prince's Risborough by four.' He flipped open his notebook. 'Oh yes, the porter said he told the garage-lads there'd been a complaint about getting the lady's car out so slow and they said it was a ruddy lie: Fellworthy had been sitting reading in the lady's car for near five minutes.'

'*Reading*? Reading what?'

'They couldn't see, but he'd got his glasses on and his head bent like he was reading.'

'You've done wonderfully well, Holmes. Thank you.'

'Pleasure, sir.'

'I wonder whether you'd do just one more thing. Could you get someone to book me on the first plane to Jersey?'

'Yessir. If the flights are full can I swing the "urgent police business" bit?' I glanced at the DCI; he hesitated, then nodded firmly.

'Need time to pack?' asked the DCI, sensibly.

'No thanks, I've plenty of gear in Jersey.'

'Car to the station?'

'Yes please. You think of everything.'

'You're not doing so bad yourself, if I may say so.'

'Kind of you. Reminds me, don't you think it'd be a good plan to warn your Information Room that if Fellworthy telephones they're not to answer any questions, just put him through to you. And if he does, and it's about the spectacles, could you stretch a point and say that they haven't turned up?'

Fifteen minutes later I was at Oxford station and, having a few minutes in hand, I dialled my own number in Jersey – the unlisted one – to warn Jock to meet me at the airport and see that there was something choice to eat. No-one answered; I vented my spleen with a few choice words to the answering machine.

XVII

A natural straight to the knave

Since that in love the pains be deadly,
Me think it best that readily
I do return to my first address;
For at this time too great is the press,
And perils appear too abundantly
For to love her.

Happy is the traveller who has no heavy luggage with him but a pocket-flask, a *Times* crossword and a firm-fitting moustache. The aeroplane was of the very latest kind but I confess I almost regretted the DC–7 of evil memory which Dryden and I had shared: I was brought up in the age of the biplane and the iron lung, I am not really at home in the age of the jet-lag and the plastic heart. I prefer the chip on my shoulder to be soggy-fried rather than silicon quartz and I cannot really believe in aircraft which are not furnished with sturdy propellers. Still, if there was nothing to fret about one wouldn't travel by air, would one?

There was a genuine taxi for hire at Jersey airport and I reached home with time in hand for a bath before dinner. Jock had returned from his dominoes Saturnalia and greeted me tactiturnly – evidently he had checked the answering machine.

'Sorry about the harsh words, Jock,' I said cheerily. 'Spoken in haste, you know. Daresay you've heard worse, eh?'

'Yeah, well, it's lucky Madam didn't check the machine, she'd have had a fit. Not that she'd have understood half them dirty words.'

'Want to bet? More to the point, what's for dinner? How is the canary? Where is my tumbler of whisky and soda? And where is Madam?'

'Nuffink; moulting; coming up; and dunno,' he replied succinctly.

'In that order?' I asked, sinking into a passing armchair.

'Yeah.'

'Then, first the whisky and soda – and go steady with the soda, I'm not made of money, you know. Some employers mark the fall of every ginger ale, did you know that? Ah, thank you, that's better. Now, pray explain all these disasters. Is the canary's moult a normal, healthy shedding of foliage such as canaries are prone to? Oh, good. And what is all this about nothing for dinner? Surely you have a little something set aside to keep up your strength? I am not proud, I shall be happy to share it with you.' He made insubordinate noises *sotto voce* until I tossed him the key to the caviar-cupboard. 'Now, what was that other thing? Ah yes, whatever do you mean when you say that you don't know where Madam is?'

'I mean like I dunno. She rung up yesterday from the Continong – France or Egypt or one of them places – asked after me health.'

'And mine, too, no doubt?'

'Well, not exackly, Mr Charlie. She only asked if you'd tidied up your face yet and I said I cooden say. I forget what else she said.'

'I'll bet you do,' I thought.

'Mind you, it isn't half coming on a treat, Mr Charlie.' I smirked.

'That's if you like having a soup-strainer hanging from your moosh.' I un-smirked.

--- - --- - --- - ---

Take my word for it, the best way to get a really good dinner is to share your thug's personal little smackerel. We kicked off with as much Beluga caviar as a fashionable Jersey dentist could earn in an hour; then, since Jock had inadvertently made far too much toast, it seemed only sensible to open a half-kilo tin of Johanna's Strasbourg Pâté de Foie Gras Truffé. Having refreshed our palates with a couple of sorbets from the deep-freeze, we made shift to stay our stomachs with a tossed endive salad, helped down with a few slices of cold roast sirloin ... but there; I must not weary you with humdrum details of our scratch indoor picnic for I am sure that you agree with me in deploring those who live for creature comforts.

The late-night movie was a bonus; Powell and Pressburger's lovely *49th Parallel*. Add a third bottle of *Antiquary* Scotch and you can well imagine that it was a tired, replete and happy Mortdecai who tottered to his blameless couch, moulting canaries and absentee wives quite forgotten for the nonce.

--- · --- · --- · ---

I shall not pretend that I awoke with a song on my lips, for I detest falsehood, but there is no doubt that, as Jock came clinking in with the tea-tray – he had selected the fortifying Earl Grey – the world seemed a ripe and juicy one. As he flung open the curtains the Jersey sun battered cheerily at the windows and I went so far as to ask Jock to open them wide. Ever thoughtful, he had placed a pair of sun-glasses on the tray; he thinks of everything.

'Did you remember to make an appointment for me with Mr Bates?' I asked confidently as the healing brew trickled in amongst my red corpuscles.

'Yeah, 'course. Said he could fit you in right after lunch. Two-fifteen. Gives you nice time to get over to St Helier for the dentist.'

'Dentist?' I quavered – the sun seemed to go into an eclipse – 'How do you mean, "dentist"? I gave no orders about dentists.'

'Madam did,' he said smugly. 'You remember; she booked you in for a check-up twice a year and today's the day. Yeah, that's it, now I remember what she said on the phone,

what I cooden remember last night. She said to make sure
you didn't forget and then she sort of laughed a bit.' He
coaxed another cup of tea into my nerveless fingers.

'Don't fret, Mr Charlie, 'sonly a check-up, he probably
won't even use the drill, let alone the pliers.' When it
comes to comforting, Job's buddies could profit from Jock's
correspondence course. 'An' your usual is by your gloves on
the hall-table.' Splendid chap, he'd remembered that I
make a practice of chewing a clove of garlic just before
visiting fashionable dentists: it cuts down your time in the
torture-chair amazingly. Try it.

Mr Bates, the orthoptist, greeted me with his usual benign
smile; he had the knack of making you feel that your visit
has made his day. He would have made an excellent bishop;
one of the good, old-fashioned sort that believes in God,
you remember.

'Well, now,' he said, after we'd exchanged felicities,
'how can I help you? Been sitting on your frames again? Or
do you need something a little stronger for reading? You
shouldn't yet, you know, if you've been doing the eye-
exercises I showed you.'

'I'm afraid it's a bit more serious than that, Mr Bates.'

'Oh dear, that's most surprising; as I recall, last year you
had normal presbyopia for a man of your age and, let me
see, a little astigmatism in the left eye. Come into the office
and let's have a look, shall we?' In the office I showed him
my temporary warrant-card and begged him – quite
unnecessarily – to keep mum. Then I showed him the
leather case.

'Goodness, yes; I remember this well, it was a very
special order indeed. It isn't often we're asked for quite such
a luxurious pair, even in Jersey. Yes, and I remember
suggesting to her husband that it might be a good idea to
put her *middle* initial on the case ... I mean, "B.F." by itself
... yes, I have the name now: Fellworthy. She came to see
me complaining of headaches and wanted to know whether
her spectacles were causing the trouble. Poor woman, I

found she had very high astigmatism in both eyes, combined with spherical errors different in each eye. Let me just get out her card. Hmm; yes, indeed. The astigmatism had not deteriorated, of course – it doesn't, you know – but she needed stronger "spheres" on both eyes and I so prescribed.

'Two minutes after she'd left, her husband came in again and said that he wanted to surprise her with something very de luxe and in high fashion: he particularly fancied those enormous circular lenses ...' I took the wrecked specs out of the case and handed them to him. 'Yes, these are they, and I remember warning him that the cost ...' His words withered away. You know how opticians, when handed a pair of glasses, hold them a few inches from their own eyes and move them back and forth? Mr Bates was doing just that when he broke off his sentence. His face went grey and, for the first time in our acquaintance, the benign smile vanished from his face.

'What in the name of ...?' he began; then turned the glasses to a vertical position and looked through the unbroken lens again. His look of shock changed to one of grim anger.

'Some infernal idiot has rotated this lens through ninety degrees,' he said, controlling his voice with an effort. 'What madman—'

'Er, no chance, I suppose, that the lens could have got loose and sort of wobbled itself round?'

'Positively not. And to *wobble*, as you put it, through precisely ninety degrees – that would be far too much of a coincidence.'

'Sorry, silly of me.'

'No-one could shift those lenses a tenth of a millimetre without using ...' – he snatched up a jeweller's loupe from his desk and screwed it into his eye – '... yes, look here!' I took the loupe and looked. 'Do you see the two tiny gold screws which clamp the rims onto the lenses? Look carefully, they're burred and scratched where someone has loosened them and then tightened them again; do you see the two sets of scratches?' I saw.

'Mr Bates,' I said soberly, 'what would be the effect on Mrs Fellworthy if she unsuspectingly put on these glasses while she was driving a car in traffic?' He thought carefully for a while, evidently trying to phrase his answer into the kind of layman's language which even I would understand.

'Try to imagine,' he said at last, 'that you are far too close to one of those huge, curved CinemaScope screens, watching a film of a motor-race. Then imagine that you are also standing on your head with your eyes crossed and blind drunk. That, roughly speaking, would be the effect. You would think that the world, or you yourself, had gone insane. If there was strong sunshine, the darkening of the lenses would make it even worse. You would, in short, be more frightened than you'd ever been in your life; the steadiest man in the world would, I should think, panic uncontrollably.' He touched the crumpled frames with gentle finger-tips. 'Is that what happened to …?'

'Yes,' I said. 'Moreover, she was in a bad state of nerves already; in fact she'd been living in terror of her life for many days before it happened.'

'Poor woman,' he murmured. He didn't ask any questions, he's not like that. I thought for a while then asked him for a stout envelope and some Scotch tape.

'Please write this on the envelope, Mr Bates: "I certify that this pair of spectacles and case were supplied by me in perfect order to Mrs Bronwen Fellworthy on such and such a date and that they are now in the exact condition as when Special Inspector Mortdecai showed them to me today, on such and such a date, signed etc." Now, I'll countersign, witnessing your signature and we'll seal all the edges and stick Scotch tape across all the writing. Thanks. Now, I must ask you to help me some more.'

I told him what I wanted. He said it would take at least a week. I said three days at the outside. 'Go to London or Paris or wherever necessary, go in person if that would help: expense is no object. You know what is involved. When you're ready, ring my home number and ask for Mr Strapp, he's my, ah, driver. He'll fly the package straight to me – I'll be in Oxford. I'll explain it all to you just as soon as I'm free to do so.'

Jock was double-parked outside. He scowled when I said that I was going to let the dentist down: I hated to disappoint him but I'd had enough violence for one day. What I needed was a sedative, such as Scotch whisky, and a telephone.

At the house and suitably sedated, I applied myself to the telephone. The DCI was off duty but I reached the excellent DC Holmes.

'Look, Holmes,' I said, 'I know this sounds a bit potty but do you think you could find out what the weather was like on that day? You know, *that* Monday. The one we were discussing yesterday.' He chuckled.

'Don't need to look that one up, sir; we'd had nigh on a month of grey sky and drizzle. It didn't let up till that particular Monday, just about lunch-time; then the sun came out a fair treat. Why I remember exactly was, it was my day off and I had to take my landlady's kids to their school Sports Day.'

'You're a ruddy marvel, Holmes,' I marvelled. 'Now, can you take down a message for the DCI, please. Top secret. Tell him our suspicions are fully confirmed, that I'll see him latish tomorrow afternoon and, yes, tell him that the good doctor was *not* reading when he was sitting in his wife's car in the hotel garage. Tell him to try that on his pianola. Right?'

'Yessir.'

I spent the rest of the afternoon and early evening congratulating myself on my infinite resource and sagacity; planning and mentally rehearsing my visit to Dr Fellworthy when the time should be ripe; whizzing through the crossword at an unprecedented speed; taking an aperitif now and then to limber up for the dinner which lay in the offing or oven; paying a duty visit to the moult-stricken feathered friend; and wondering whether Johanna would telephone. She didn't, of course; they never do, do they?

Dinner, however, healed all wounds and since I was doomed to an indefinite number of Scone High Table's poisoned pottages, I allowed myself, for once, to eat heartily, like some dromedary ship of the desert tanking up at an oasis. (Not, I hasten to say, that I actually drank any water: I never do, you don't know where it's been.)

I took Vol. IV of Gibbon's *Decline and Fall of the Roman Empire* to bed with me and in no time I was sleeping righteously.

XVIII

Dealer shows his hand

Throughout the world, if it were sought,
Fair words enough a man shall find:
They be good cheap, they cost right nought.
Their substance is but only wind:
But well to say and so to mean,
That sweet accord is seldom seen.

'Jock,' I said to the grizzled retainer as he lowered the tea-tray onto my unwilling lap the next morning, 'look me in the eye if you dare! Is this your idea of gratitude for my keeping you out of the nick all these years? You know jolly well that reveille in this bedroom is at 11 a.m. I'm prepared to offer long odds that it is now little more than 10 ditto. What do you mean by harrying me out of blameless slumber in the grey light of dawn? Eh?'

'Sorry, Mr Charlie, I cooden book you on the after-lunch flight, it's full up, so I had to get you on the 12.05. You check in at 11.30.'

'My God!' I cried, aghast, 'my luncheon …!'

' 'Salright, Mr Charlie, Cookie's packed you a lovely lunch: 'arf a chicken, 'arf a dozen gull's eggs, 'arf a bottle of white Burgundy and 'arf a pound of Mr B.'s special shooting-cake.'

'Oh, very well,' I hmphed, 'I suppose I can rough it for once. We old campaigners, you know … but see that there is a sustaining breakfast ready for me in twenty-five minutes. And fill the larger of my pocket-flasks.'

'Right, Mr Charlie.'

'Carry on, Jock.'

As he drove me to the airport I said, 'Jock, lend me your ears.'

'Yer what?'

'I mean, pay attention carefully; memorise the following as though it were the Judges' Rules: as soon as you have shovelled me onto the aircraft you are to proceed to Bellingham's courteous travel agency – let me see, it's the 15th inst., right? – and book yourself on a late afternoon flight to Heathrow or Gatwick on the 17th and the three following days. During that period – the 17th until the 20th – you must at all costs stay within earshot of the telephone until, let's say, 6 p.m. On one of those days, probably the first of them, Mr Bates, the amiable eye-ball engineer whom I visited yesterday, will phone, asking for you by name and saying that all is ready. You will throw your overnight-bag into the car and make all speed to Mr Bates, who will hand you a package. Hop on the plane, make your way to Oxford and go straight to the cop-shop (oh, do keep your eyes on the road, Jock and stop boggling – this cop-shop will do you no harm, I swear, they won't even take your fingerprints). At the said cop-shop you will hand the packet personally to the Detective Chief Inspector or to a Detective Constable called Holmes. It is better that you do not attempt to get in touch with me; it would be *insecure*. Take a room in some modestly priced Temperance Hotel suitable to your station in life, talk to no-one, and do not, on any account, get into any bar-room brawls. Then make your way back to Jersey first thing in the morning. Right, Jock?'

'Right, Mr Charlie.' I gave him some money, enough to keep him out of trouble but not enough to get him into any.

At Oxford station there were, needless to say, no taxis to be had. What there was, however, was a shiny black limousine and a uniformed copper holding the door open for me. Long and bitter experience has given me a rooted distrust of shiny black limousines so I startled the driver by asking for his warrant-card. Well, I'd rather be taken for a twit by a genuine policeman than taken for a ride by a bogus one, wouldn't you?

'However did you know I'd be on this train?' I asked as we drifted toward Christ Church.

'DC Holmes figured it out, sir. Lovely set of brains he's got. Nice with it too. Even with villains, unless they get above themselves.'

'And then?'

'Gives them a little friendly lesson in karate. He's got one of them black belts. Never leaves a mark on 'em, either.'

———————

The DCI beamed at me across his desk, but it was the beam of a man who has just been munching a moody fingernail.

'Well, well, well!' I cried heartily. 'Did you work out what Dr F. was doing when he wasn't reading in his wife's car?'

'Yes.'

My face fell disappointedly.

The DCI seemed to be battling with his conscience. 'Well,' he said finally, 'I didn't actually figure it out myself; it was DC Holmes. He reckons Fellworthy was, as he puts it, frigging with his wife's glasses.'

'My word! Is there no end to that chap's resourcefulness?' And then, to salve his pride, 'I must say you train your squad admirably, Chief Inspector.'

'Thank you, most kind; we try to do our best. But what about those bloody glasses?'

'Look, before we start, I'd better say that what I've got in mind is possibly going to need the assistance of a real policeman – and possibly one who can use a little tactful violence. I wondered whether you'd consider sort of putting Holmes on stand-by call for me if I should need him. It would hardly interfere with his usual duties – just an hour or so at odd times during the next ten days or so …?'

'You couldn't have picked a better man,' he said handsomely. 'He's got brains, brawn and balls – like the ideal President the Americans never get.'

'Is he close-mouthed?'

'A veritable oyster.'

'Then I suggest we have him in, now, so that he's in the picture. Might do the wrong thing if he didn't know what it was all about.' He gnawed a nail or two, then intercommed. DC Holmes clockwork-soldiered in, was told to sit.

'Look here, young Holmes,' said the DCI, 'this is so confidential that I'm putting myself at risk letting you in on it. To put it bluntly, we common jacks have been warned off the Fellworthy case by some conniving political pignuts. BUT I'M NOT HAVING MURDER GOT AWAY WITH IN MY BLOODY MANOR! The Chief Constable feels the same way as I do, which is why he's demi-officially given Special Inspector Mortdecai a brief to dig around tactfully. By giving him assistance I'm disobeying my orders from Whitehall. Right, I've put my head on the block – if you want to shop me you can have me in charge of traffic-control on the Norfolk Broads next week. I don't think you're that kind of a man.'

'Correct, sir. I call it a compliment you trusting me, sir. And anyway, if I did the dirty on you I'd never be trusted by anyone in the Force again, would I?' The DCI chuckled.

'Yes, I thought that would occur to you. By the way, I believe you passed your Detective Sergeant's exams?'

'Yessir. Twice, sir.' The unspoken promise floated delicately to the floor between them.

'Right, Mr Mortdecai. Now tell us.'

'First,' I said, plonking the envelope on his desk, 'these are the mortal remains of Bronwen's glasses, exactly as you gave them to me but now, as you see, sealed up, certified by the optician who prescribed and fitted them and counter-signed by Special Inspector Me. Now, sir—' He raised a protesting hand – all sirring had hitherto been in the other direction.

'Well, look,' I said, 'you are my, ah, demi-official superior now and I can't keep calling you "Detective Chief Inspector," it makes my tongue ache. What would one of your own Inspectors call you?'

' "Chief" usually. Only "sir" if I was giving him a going-over.'

'Right, Chief. And please call me Charlie. You,' I said, turning to Holmes sternly, 'may continue to call me "sir."'

'Yessir,' he said. The momentary twinkle in his eye was by no means insubordinate.

'Now, Chief,' I continued, 'I submit that you might care to date-stamp this envelope, initial the stamp and pop the whole thing into your safest safe. We shan't need it until the trial.'

'But won't you need to take the glasses with you when you visit Fellworthy?'

'I'll be coming to that presently. Now, this is how the murder was committed ...' and I told them all. Well, almost all. Certainly all that was good for them. When I had finished, I summed it all up incisively: 'Well,' I said, 'and there you are, aren't you?'

Holmes looked at me applaudingly but said, 'Bloody twit. They're all the same, aren't they, sir?' He was addressing the DCI and I bridled for a moment.

'Yes,' said the DCI heavily, 'they're all the same. Villain does a lovely £50,000 job with a thermic lance – no dabs, a new *modus operandio*, nothing for us to go on at all. Next week he buys his tart a mink, and bing-bong-willy-wong, we've got him. Same as this Fellworthy: perfect murder, Crime of the Century, no-one would ever know it *was* a murder even, but he has to—' I broke in courteously:

'He has to draw your attention to himself by making a fuss about the wretched glasses and arouse your suspicions, Chief, eh?' He shot me a furtively grateful glance.

'Right,' he said. 'If he'd never mentioned them he'd have got them back by now. Rightly does DC Holmes call him a twit. When I think of all that ingenuity going into his caper and then it all being spoiled by mere human frailty – well, it makes me despair of criminal nature.'

'Amateurs,' murmured Holmes.

'Even the pros are amateurs,' snapped the DCI; '*we're* the only professionals, we do it for a living. Villains make a quick tickle, laughing their heads off at Old Bill, then spend ten years in the slammer, thinking up another caper.' He turned to me. 'We sent a bloke "up the stairs" – that's our vulgar way of saying The Old Bailey – last month. He drew "During her Majesty's Pleasure." Fifty years old and he's spent twenty-five of them in the nick. Probably *still* thinks he's smart.'

'Ah well, Chief,' I said, trying to lighten his mood, 'this was a one-off job and you've got him, ah, dead to rights, haven't you, what?'

'No,' he said morosely.

'*No*?'

'No. First, I've had orders from On High to leave the whole mess alone, as you well know. Oh, I could bash it through all right, 'specially now the political thing turns out to be a load of old moody, but it'd still be me for the Norfolk Broads. My missus has these lovely long legs, you see,' he went on irrelevantly, 'and she can't bear gumboots.' I tried once again, in my foolish way, to lighten his mood.

'Never marry a woman with lovely long legs, Chief, she's liable to walk out on you, hah hah ...'

'So could one with ugly short legs,' said the logical Holmes.

'Ah, but who would *care*?'

The intercom buzzed and a female voice, evidently coming from a mouth full of hairpins, said that Dr Fellworthy wished to speak to the DCI. Chiefy arranged his features, adopted an unctuous voice.

'No, Doctor, the spectacles under advisement have not yet emerged to the surface, as you might say, but I have two men, *pro bono* as we say, checking pawnshops, old-gold dealers and such this very minute.' He span the dial an inch, to give the impression that he was making a connection to the Information Room, then scowled and winked hideously at Holmes.

'Sergeant!' he barked, 'any word yet on the pair of lady's gold-rimmed glasses?' Holmes – what an admirable man! – turned away, stuck two fingers in his mouth and bellowed. 'Not yet, sir, but we have high hopes. We covered all likelies in the city centre; moving into outlying suburbs tomorrow. Reckon they must be in the vicinity: not enough gold to peddle them in London. They'll turn up, sir.'

'Are you still there, Doctor?' soaped the DCI. 'We are confident of finding your dear departed's *memento moria*; I realise how much such small relicts mean to a bereaved person. Yes, sir, I understand perfectly ... yes ... yes ... and I hope you are bearing up, sir; always bear in mind that these things are sent to try us, aren't they?' As he put the telephone back on its cradle he homed in on my quizzical eyebrows. 'Oh, shit,' he said, 'that last sentence was a bit inopportune, wasn't it?' I shrugged. He pulled himself together.

'Now,' he said, 'as I was about to say before DC Holmes brought up the subject of my lady-wife's limbs, the second factor is that there just isn't enough evidence to offer a court. He wouldn't even need a barrister; any smart-arse from a cut-price Legal Clinic would get it chucked out at the Magistrate's Hearing.'

'But but but,' I said lucidly, 'but but but! I mean, dash it! Look, we've got Means: the murder weapon or deodand is on your very desk in that envelope. We've got Opportunity: the five furtive minutes in Bronwen's bucket-seat in the hotel garage. We've got his insistence on circular lenses from the optician; we've got her irrational fears about Reds under her herring which were supposed to throw us off the scent; and we've got Motive.'

'What motive?'

'Oh, come *on*, Chief; every married man has an occasional desire to murder his wife, this is common knowledge. I mean, that's what meat-cleavers are for, isn't ...' I tailed off, for I realised that I was in the midst of a gritty sort of silence; the silence of a gravel drive which no-one is walking on. My hand, unbidden, flew to my moustache.

'What I mean,' I gabbled, 'what I mean, of course, is that *separated* married couples have a lot of stresses and strains, and, ah, strains and, well, stresses. I mean, one of them wants to give it another try, perhaps, while the other is intent on a full divorce.' By sheer will-power I forced my hand away from the guilty apple-orchard of my upper lip. The silence went on, more benignly now, but I was damned if I was going to be the first to break it. I like silences, I cultivate and collect them, but I mutely prayed to whomever might be listening that someone would say something. I should have remembered the only sensible thing St Teresa ever said: 'It is those of our prayers which are answered which cause us to shed tears.'

'Tell him, Holmes,' said the DCI.

'DCI's right, sir. You couldn't shop a Liberal MP on that evidence these days. Like he says, it'd hardly get past the Magistrate's Ear-ring. Mind you, if Fellworthy was smart, he'd elect for trial by jury and get a top "brief." At quarter-sessions, right after the prosecutor's openers, the "brief" would get up and submit there was no case to answer. The judge (the good old bloodthirsty breed is all dead or retired now) would so instruct the jury. Jury'd be packed with women – and you know women think that doctors are the nearest thing to God ...' The DCI broke in:

'Good thinking, Holmes; once he was acquitted in full court he couldn't be tried again for the murder, no matter what evidence we might find afterwards. He could walk around shouting "I done it, I done it" and we could only touch him for Disorderly Behaviour. No Charlie, we've got to have something more. If we can't get his neck for sure ...'

'... they'll have yours,' I said. 'Very well; I've got a bit of a ploy in mind. Take notes, please, Holmes. "A" – have you written that down? Good. "A:" in a few days from now a large, ugly man with a glass eye will appear at the counter of this cop-shop. He will be carrying a package to be delivered to the DCI or, should the DCI be out for lunch, to you. He will hand it to no-one else. Pray tell all of your colleagues who might be on duty at the cash-desk that he will be about his lawful occasions. You see, he is, even to the untrained eye, a member of the criminal classes and it is important that he should be neither molested nor harassed. He answers to the name of Mr Strapp. His only fault is that he dearly loves to hit people, especially uniformed ones, and, strange as it may seem, he's afraid of no-one but me.' Holmes gave me one of those long, careful looks which only good policemen know how to give.

'I wouldn't say that was all that strange, sir.' I almost blushed; my silly-arse mask must have slipped a little.

'Chhrrmm,' I said. 'What I mean is, see that he is allowed to hand the package by hand, so to say, to the DCI or yourself and that no-one gives him any "aggro." His skin is exceptionally sensitive and exhibits a strong allergy to fingerprint-ink. He will leave Oxford by the next town drain, I assure you. Do I make myself clear?'

'Abundantly, sir. Indeed, I'll see that he's given a cup of tea.'

'Oh dear no, I wouldn't do that, really. No stimulants. Just let him go in peace. Now, Chief,' I turned to the Chief, 'this package must be passed to me at Scone College – hand to hand – just as soon as human foot or car can convey it. Will you see to that, please? This is of the *essence*, as French motorists say.'

'Right.'

'Next, "B:" what sort of jurisdiction or influence do you have amongst your country colleagues in Dr Fellworthy's bit of Buckinghamshire, eh?'

'Ah, well, sir – sorry – Charlie, that point is a bit moot. In fact I'd say it was highly moot. I mean, we're all Thames Valley Police nowadays and we take turns manning the Regional Crime Squad and that, but old habits die hard. Like, if some jack from Thame came clumping into our manor in hot pursuit of a shop-lifter, he'd get a root up the sump, see? I mean, we collaborate amicably. Like Stalin and Churchill.'

'Oh dear,' I said. In fact I said 'Oh dear' again, for this made my plans look like a plate of ill-forked spaghetti.

'Anyway,' said the DCI, 'what do you want a lot of Bucks. flatties in muddy wellies clumping about with you for? You've got DC Holmes, haven't you? You're only going to see one inoffensive murderer tomorrow, right?'

'Well, no, not tomorrow really. I'm not going to see the Dr until the aforementioned package arrives; you can see that, I'm sure. I just want to do a bit of snooping and sleuthing while I wait for it.' Holmes breathed in and out in a respectful way. The DCI made a noise like a bull-terrier with catarrh.

'Special Inspector Mortdecai,' he said, in just those saccharine tones that a Princess uses to a press photographer at a puissance trial, 'I am well aware that your brains are big enough to stuff a goose with – from either end – but I do think that AS YOUR FUCKING SUPERIOR OFFICER it is high time you let me in on all this roly-moly about mysterious packages and, and – all that.'

'Oh, dammit, Chief, I'm awfully sorry; I'm not a trained policeman, you know that, haven't put the facts in the right order. This is what I had in mind.' I told them what I had in mind. When it was in his mind it churned around a little, then he nodded. It was an almost entirely ungrudging nod, as nods go – and I reckon myself a pretty good judge of a nod.

'Going back to the Bucks. alleged Constabulary,' he said, 'despite my previous remarks I should point out that, although I have nothing that you could call hegemony over that, er, admirable body of men, it does just so happen that my brother-in-law is the Superintendent at Prince's Risborough. Married to my sister,' he explained.

'How nice,' I said. He gave me an odd look.

'She is a Primitive Baptist; her husband drinks beer and has been seen playing darts on Sunday.'

'Whew!' I said.

'But she loves her brother: me, see? So any little favour he can do for me becomes a pleasure and a privilege for him. I'll ring him in a minute, tell him that a, a, a Trusted Subordinate of mine will be calling on him first thing in the morning. Right?'

'Splendid,' I said, 'very kind. Just one thing, though: "first thing in the morning" might mean anything really, mightn't it. And I'm not what you'd call a dedicated early riser – often up with the lark, yes, but only when I'm on my way home to bed. Suppose we say "first thing after lunch," eh? Catch him in the well-known post-prandial glow, d'you see? And if it wouldn't interfere with your duty-roster too much, perhaps DC Holmes could wheel me over there; then, while I'm chatting up your bro-in-law the Super, Holmes could be collecting a bit of back-stairs stuff from the rank and file in the Duty Room over a dish of tea – you know, the sort of stuff which might not have filtered up to the higher echelons, so to say, eh? The gossip I mean, not the tea.'

He gave me a 'righto' and a 'good luck' or two and I thank-you'd my way out.

So content was I with my sleuthing and my cunning plans that a younger, less pompous sleuth would have stuck his hands in his pockets and whistled a jaunty air. Foolish, hubristic Mortdecai, little did you guess how the jealous gods were even then spitting on their hands and rolling up their sleeves, preparing a world-overturning wallop for you, to be collected at the very Porter's Lodge itself.

XIX

Second red queen shows

In faith I wot not well what to say,
Thy chances been so wonderous;
Thou Fortune with thy diverse play
That causeth joy full dolorous.

'Er, Mr Mortdecai,' muttered the Porter as I passed into the Lodge archway.

'Yes, Fred?' I answered courteously.

'That horse ...'

'Finished last, eh? Don't give it another thought.'

'Well, to tell the truth, sir, I put your winnings on something which could hardly stand up, like you said, but it come up mud.'

'Sorry, Fred, you'll have to translate.'

'Well, it rained, see, in the morning, like, and they nearly called the meeting off but they never. The course was like Shit Creek by the fifth race.'

'Dear me,' I said absently, 'and I suppose they called it off, what?'

'Well, not the fifth they didn't. And it turns out your horse was 'arf-brother to an 'ippopotamouse, loves mud; bred in Cambridge I reckon ...' The awful truth advanced.

'Fred, are you trying to tell me ...?'

'Yes, Mr Mortdecai. 'E romps home while the rest of the field are blowing bleeding bubbles. I'm sorry, I never knew, did I? Or I'd've 'ad a few bob on meself, wouldn't I?' I seethed; I do not *like* having the Eternal Scheme of Things turned upsy-down at the whim of an equine mud-lark.

'Fred,' I gritted, 'this time let there be no mistake; deduct a handsome commission for your trouble, then put these winnings onto a horse guaranteed to have the botts, the glanders, the stifles and the spavins, break its leg with your own hands if necessary, but let your next bulletin tell of a resounding loss. Is that clear?'

'Yes, sir. Oh, Turner is off duty tomorrow, I'll tell the other bloke you want tea at 10.30, right?'

'Right, Fred.'

I forget what we had for dinner at High Table. I *choose* to forget. Dryden was busy decocting an examination paper so I repaired to Bronwen's set, booted the accursed pink piggy-wig downstairs yet again and went to bed with a pipkin of Scotch for my stomach's sake (First Epistle of Paul to Timothy, V:23 – one of the few points on which Paul and I see eye to eye) and Bronwen's copy of Douglas's *Old Calabria*, that grossly neglected masterpiece, now in several masterful pieces, thanks to my recent visitors.

— · — · — · — · — · — · —

If you cannot trust a senior Scone scout, whom can you trust? I know all about industrial unrest, nuclear devices, the *Untergang des Abendlandes*, Women's Liberation and other threats to civilisation-as-we-know-it, but none of these is an excuse for the cup of tepid slurry which was dumped on my bedside table the next morning.

'Hoy!' I croaked at the vanishing scout as soon as I had sprayed out the preliminary sip. He returned, puzzled.

'Did you say "hoy," sir?'

'Yes, I did jolly well say "hoy," although it is a word I seldom use. I distinctly recall ordering tea; this potation tastes of cocoa, dammit!'

'Sorry, sir; if it tastes of cocoa I must have brought you the coffee by mistake.' I eyed him dangerously but decided that he was not jesting. The tea, when it arrived, would have delighted 'the old man of Peru, Who dined upon vegetable stew,' but it held no charm for me. I tugged on a garment or two and shuffled crossly to Broad Street, where there is still a place at which the better kind of Balliol undergraduate can order breakfast in his dressing-gown and bedroom-slippers. The waitress – 'nourrie dans le sérail' – could tell at a glance that I was neither a Balliol man nor any kind of under-graduate, but she knew a Charvet dressing-gown when she saw one and the tea and richly buttered toast which she brought me would have earned a grunt of approval from Jock himself.

Later, dressed, shaven and otherwise fortified, I was in good mid-season form to greet DC Holmes when he swept discreetly up to the Porter's Lodge in a discreetly plain-clothed motorcar.

'Holmes,' I said as we swooped towards leafy Bucks., 'there is a testing task before you; steel yourself. Whilst I am upstairs in this rural cop-shop, making myself agreeable to the Superintendent, you will be on the Lower Deck, so to say, courteously accepting mugs of strong tea from the gum-booted arms of the Buckinghamshire law. Right?'

'Yessir,' he said; yes, there was a trace not of mutiny but of discontent in that 'yessir:' the sort of controlled discomfort of a hen laying a square egg.

'No, look here, Holmes, it's important: swallow your pride, be gracious to these country cousins and, when your lofty condescension has warmed their hearts, get the dirt from them. Anything at all about Dr Fellworthy, omitting no nuance however slight. Find, if you can, some rustic malcontent, some uniformed oaf, who blames the professional classes for all his own shortcomings; he'll be the chap ... but I'm sure you need no guidance from me.'

'Yessir,' he said, emitting no nuance however slight. How he forbore to call me "Watson" I shall never know; he must have been a man of iron.

The Superintendent or brother-in-law kept me waiting just ninety seconds; a good sign. He rose to greet me: another good sign. I briefly flashed a selected credential or two and he instantly offered me a cigarette. Any ethologist could have told that the pecking-order was clearly marked out.

As I had hoped, he bore all the signs of a man who has enjoyed his lunch. He bore, too, a confident, dominant, fearless aspect such as do all men who have to become hen-pecked cravens the moment they return to their lovely homes.

'Dr Fellworthy,' I said crisply.

'Eh?' said the Super with equal crispness. 'Oh, *that's* what it's about, is it? Dr Fellworthy. Yes, very nice gentleman. Shocking tragedy, shocking. As it happens, I handled the case myself.'

Any cartoonist would have seen a well-defined '!' emerging in a bubble from my head.

'Yes,' he went on, 'I was a mere Sergeant at the time.'

The bubble stretched to bursting-point, it was now a ghetto of '!'s and '?'s. I reached into the scrambled eggs of what had been my brains and picked out a solid bit.

'Super!' I said. 'No, no, I don't mean "super," sorry, I mean "Super" – as in "intendent," you understand.' He looked at me in an odd sort of way.

'Superintendent,' I said, 'could we sort of start again? For instance, are we talking about W.W. Fellworthy, MD (Oxon), of this parish, widower?'

'Yes.'

'Who lost his wife in a shocking car accident?'

'Yes.'

'And you've made Sergeant to Superintendent in those dozen or so days since the Tragedy?'

'Eight or nine *years*,' he said gently. I resisted the temptation to beat my head against the edge of his desk; chaps with haughty moustaches must live up to them, you see. The Super pressed a buzzer on his desk and I whirled around, prepared to resist any male nurses in white coats who might enter with plain vans tucked under their arms.

What entered, in fact, was a monstrous, dark-blue bosom, followed some ten inches later by its owner, the most terrifying policewoman I've ever seen. When I say that Jock himself would not have liked to encounter her in some dark alley I think I have said it all. The Super didn't seem in the least frightened of her, although her spade-like hands hung down to her knees.

'Petal,' he said, 'file on Fellworthy; *fast*.' I do think that at this point he might have offered me a drink. Petal was back in a twinkling (although I realise that's an inept word), slapped a slim file onto the Super's desk and hovered officiously. 'Hop it,' he said. My respect for the man grew.

'Rrrr,' he said as he thumbed through the file, 'yes, Agnes Hortense Fellworthy. Yes, just eight years and two months ago. Shocking.' My eggy brain slowly unscrambled itself and an omelette began to form: *baveuse* or gooey in the middle but none the worse for that. Having borne with fortitude the news that Miss Fellworthy was, in fact, *Mrs* ditto, it was not too hard to take the tidings that there was now a brace of Mrs F.s. I phrased my question with care.

'When you say "shocking," Super, how do you mean? "Shocking," I mean.'

'Drettful,' he explained. 'Lovely lady, she was, I met her often. Drove out one afternoon for the shopping, down the drive, straight across the main road, right through the middle of a Cycling Club outing, through a quickset hedge and precipitated herself and vehicle over, well, a precipice. Hundred and fifty feet.'

'Died instantaneously, I suppose?'

'Well, no-one hardly ever walks away from a mischance of that sort, sir. Especially if your vehicle becomes a blazing holocaust as it strikes the bottom of the quarry.' For my part I knew that I had struck pay-dirt: the nuggets of gold glistered before my eyes.

'She was, of course, wearing her spectacles at the time?'

'Eh? No, never wore them.' My nuggets became fool's gold and the iron pyrites entered into my soul.

'But sun-glasses, surely,' I whined. He thought ponderously, wetted a thumb and leafed through the file.

'No. One of the Cycling Club, whom she narrowly missed killing, states that her eyes were wide open, staring straight ahead.'

'Post-mortem?'

'Naturally. Trace of alcohol, consistent with one sherry before lunch, confirmed by her husband. No trace of any drug or medicine. The coroner unhesitatingly returned "Accidental." Oh, yes, I see that her own doctor, at the inquest, deposed that he had warned her against driving fast on account of being liable to short black-outs, her being pregnant, if you'll excuse the expression.'

'And was she?'

'Well, no, the post-mortem didn't show anything of that.'

'But the doc in question said that she was, ah, expecting?'

'No, he didn't exactly say that, he used the term "*petit male*," you know what these doctors are for fancy terms.'

'Yes, indeed. Could I have the name and address of this doctor, please?'

It was four o'clock; that fearful hour when vicars' wives and policemen take tea, a fluid which is necessary at dawn but positively harmful at other times. I declined the cup which was pressed upon me; when you have drunk one cop-shop cup of tea you have drunk them all. More to the point, when one is nurturing a lusty young chrysanthemum on the upper lip it is important to avoid nitrogenous stimulants. (I once knew a chap in the Royal West African Frontier Force who cured himself of a tiresome little infestation by soaking his pubic hair with paraffin and touching a match to it. The infestation perished; so did his marriage.)

Down in the dungeon department I found Holmes quaffing that very liquid (tea, of course, not paraffin – I must try to be more lucid) with the pongid Petal and many an amply-booted he-copper. We drove away in the general direction of Oxford. After a few minutes he said, 'Sir, I'm slowing down. On your right you'll see where the original Mrs Fellworthy went to meet her Maker in the quarry and on your left you'll see the Fellworthy domicile.' The left was what interested me; a long, straight drive, leading straight down to the road and trimmed, on the western side only, by a high fence, like one of those flashy picket-fences you see around those places which want to look like stud-farms, but higher and with the upright posts closer together. It was not sightly, nor did I much like the look of the long, low house which squatted at the summit of the drive. Perhaps it was because there was a good chance that a murderer was even then peering at us from one of the windows. I have no especial grudge against murderers – they go their way and I go mine – but I confess that I don't much like the thought of them looking at me thoughtfully.

'Holmes,' I said thoughtfully as the car picked up speed, 'at what time today would you normally have ceased duty and returned to your nearest and dearest?'

'Four o'clock, sir. But it's all right, I'm quite enjoying myself and there's no hurry. And my nearest and dearest is a norrible old landlady who sniffs me breath every time I come in and pushes leaflets under me door about Demon Drink.'

'Once again you have gone to the heart of the matter, Holmes, your instincts are unerring. You see, I wished to know whether or not you were officially off duty. Plainly, you are. I wished to ascertain whether you were a dedicated teetotaller. Plainly, you are not. If you will pull into a suitably quiet road-side spot I should much like to show you a most capacious silver pocket-flask engraved with a veritable triumph of Edwardian technology.'

After the flask had passed between us a few times, with many a musical 'glug,' I told him what I had learnt and invited his contribution to the seminar.

'Get any dirty?' is how I put it to him.

'Yessir. And I don't mean the tea in the canteen, ha ha.'

'You should try the sherry in the Senior Common Room at Scone, ha ha.'

On the strength of that brace of witticisms I fished out the capacious flask again and we supped, offering mute thanks to Allah, who made men hollow.

'First, sir, I've had a word with the Sergeant who examined the charred vehicle in which the first Mrs Fellworthy met her end. He is a car buff and assured me categorically that the brakes, steering-linkages and all that had not been tampered with. He took particular interest in this scrutiny because he happens to hate the guts of Dr F. and would dearly have liked to feel his collar.'

'Why?'

'I'll be coming to that. Second, the first Mrs Fellworthy, as you already ascertained, never wore glasses of any shape or form. Third, she was abstemious in her own habits but generous with liquor to guests, passing policemen, postmen and such.'

I know a hint when I hear one: I passed the flask.

'Fourth, although somewhat older than Dr F., she was a lovely lady and anyone could tell she loved her husband. Doted on him, in fact, despite his occasional insensate rages.'

'Insensate rages?' I said, pricking up the ears.

'I'll be coming to that, sir. Sixth—'

'Sorry, shouldn't that have been "fifth," Holmes?' He counted on his fingers and agreed.

'Fifth, she was a rich or wealthy lady. She and him had a joint account at Martin's Bank, Prince's Risborough, which he occasionally used, but most of the heavy bills were paid by the lady, using an account with a London bank which I was not able to ascertain the name of.'

'Ho ho!' I thought to myself – well, I could hardly have been thinking to anyone else, could I? – 'This has all the savour of the true argol or yak-turd.'

'And …?' I murmured coaxingly.

'*Sixth*, I formed the opinion that Fellworthy is stark, staring fucking bonkers. Believed to be "suffering from mental abnormality," as we say in the Force.'

'Goodness, Holmes, did the Bucks. flatties tell you that, "in their own words," as you say in the Force?'

'Yessir. Well, they rabbitted on about our client's general deportment and demeanour and I made the inference from the signs and symptoms described. I have been studying Forensic Psychology for my Inspector's Examination, you see.'

'I see.'

'That's if I ever get my sodding Sergeant's stripes,' he added bitterly.

'Holmes,' I said, 'it is clear to the meanest intelligence that you are a man of destiny. If – in this order – I; the

Chief Constable of Oxfordshire; the Warden of Scone; and Heaven have any say in the matter, those stripes shall shortly be glistering upon your sleeve like jewels in an Ethiop's ear. Particularly since your own DCI will soon be bashfully taking the credit for solving not one but two fiendish murders, unaided by human hand such as yours and mine. I'm sure you follow me?'

'Yessir,' he said.

'Now; the reasoning behind your inference that Dr Fellworthy is potty?'

'Insensate rages, like I said; but switching instantaneously, at will, to calm normality and charm. Classic schizo and paranoiac pattern. Like, one moment a bloke is chasing his wife with a meat-axe, frothing at the mouth; next moment, when the police and doctors arrive, he's relaxed in an armchair, offering sherry, apologising that his wife called them out and hinting that she's having a bad menopause. Classic.'

'Hmm. Particular examples in this case?'

'Yessir. Stopped for speeding once; cursed and screamed at the motorcycle officer in a demented way. Patrol car pulls up and he greets the officers matily, offers to submit to the breathalyser (no reaction) and says that he probably *was* going a bit over the speed limit; thought the officer who stopped him was one of them Hell's Angels. In court next week, perfect performance as a good citizen; had had a hard day, everything going wrong – *you* know – regrets if he expressed himself a little freely to the officer; sorry to take up the court's time etc., etc. Not a dry eye in the house. Not a stain on his character. On the way home, stops at the greengrocer's and froths at the mouth horribly because they haven't got any fresh lettuce.'

'Surely, you mean the *chemist's*, Holmes?'

'No, sir, it was a fresh lettuce he wanted, not—'

'Sorry, go on. The image of a psychopathic personality does seem to emerge. Dip into the bag again.'

'Well, that fence you seen on the side of his drive. Frenzied he was about that. Frenzied. His gardener reckoned that half the number of posts would do the work and look better: he used horrible language at the gardener, sacked him on the spot. Same evening, he goes round to the gardener's cottage, gives him a bottle of Scotch and three months' wages and hopes there's no hard feelings. Gardener accepts the wages, rejects the Scotch (being teetotal) and tells Dr F. to F. off.' Something stirred in the Mortdecai brain-pan, just the first faint 'blup' of half-awakened porridge but an unmistakable 'blup.'

XX

Third queen books a loser

Comfort thyself my woeful heart,
Resound ye woods and hear your fill.
Alas, the grief and deadly doleful smart!

It may be well, like it who will.
Grudge on who list, this is my part.

A second viewing failed to heighten my opinion of the
Fellworthy mansion. Long and flat and immaculately
featureless, it had obviously been erected by an anally
retentive dwarf with a low-grade O level in Lego.

'Never trust a gentleman who lives in a bungalow, sir,'
said Holmes, as we sailed up the drive, passing the
hideous fence.

'At least he'll never be able to dress up as his dear
deceased Mama and throw prowlers headlong down the
stairs,' I riposted, recalling the fate of the poor detective
who took a tumble at the Bates Motel.

'Very true, sir.' Holmes was the ideal travelling
companion, always bowing to one's better judgement.

Beside the front door, a bronze plaque carried an
inscription that seemed to confirm earlier reports of the
somewhat schizophrenic nature of Dr Fellworthy's
personality. "W.W. Fellworthy, MD (Oxon), FRCP, FRS" it
read, "Trespassers Will Be Taken Care Of."

Before ringing the bell, I took the opportunity to spy through the spy-hole. I was met by another eye, spying back at me. The alien eye disappeared, there was the ostentatious sound of the unhooking of chains and the front door swung open while I was still bent double. The man who greeted us was as neat as a new pin, and nearly as lean. His face was so spruce that it might have been cleaned and scrubbed on a daily basis, employing only the spittle of young aristocrats. A pair of pince-nez was clipped onto a nose as sharp and ruthless as a kitchen appliance. But my eyes locked on to the feature that seemed to crawl along his upper lip like a worm dipped in soot. Never has a moustache been more like an eyebrow, and a well-plucked eyebrow at that. Had it been any skimpier, it might have doubled as a coastal footpath on an Ordnance Survey map.

'How very good of you to come, Mr, ah ...' said the doctor, outstretching a well-polished paw. I watched as his eyes hovered in envy over my infinitely more luxuriant and manly meadow.

'Mortdecai,' I said. 'The Honourable Charlie. My father was er ... yes ... hmm ...' I sometimes feel it appropriate to drop the odd clue to my aristocratic credentials. 'And this is my young assistant, Detective Constable Holmes.'

'Come in, gentlemen, come in!' Fellworthy made an elaborate display of wiping his spotless shoes on the doormat, even though he had not been outside. Holmes and I took the hint and followed suit. I watched as six brisk swipes of Holmes's shoes saw hairs of brush fly all over the shop and great arid valleys of nothingness appear upon the mat. Holmes was a solidly-built man who clearly put his black belt in karate to good use in even the most mundane of household tasks.

Fellworthy appeared not to notice the absconding bristles as they jetted haphazardly this way and that, though I fancy I saw his wormy moustache slither vainly in protest, even as his mouth busily choreographed itself into an ingratiating smile.

I decided to set the man at his ease with a bit of idle chat. 'I couldn't help but notice that you have a moustache hidden on your face, Doctor,' I began. 'Just above the lip, if I'm not mistaken. May I ask you how long have you been attempting to cultivate it?'

Fellworthy didn't miss a beat. 'How very kind of you to ask, Mr Mortdecai,' he replied. 'I have been the owner of a moustache for twenty-three years.'

'Twenty-three years,' I sighed compassionately, 'and still little bigger than a beansprout.' I lovingly stroked my own great rainforest, now so luxuriant that a well-planned expedition into its interior might well have found Mr Kurtz and chums exchanging pleasantries at its very heart. 'It might be time to start thinking of growing another one alongside it. The poor wee thing looks so very, very lonely. It could do with a little friend to keep it company. They could hold hands, sing songs and keep each other warm during those long winter nights.'

During the course of my sage advice, the doctor developed a nervous twitch that began to play havoc with his frozen smile. 'You are, I believe, here on business, gentlemen,' he twitched, removing his pince-nez and placing them on one of those tables best suited to hosting a TV dinner. 'You will understand that my time is ... er ... limited. Not to mention, ahem, costly.'

'You will be delighted to hear, Dr Fellworthy,' I said, dipping into my coat pocket, 'that we have managed to retrieve the spectacles of your late wife.'

His hand darted towards the glasses-case like a peckish python towards a passing bunny-rabbit. 'How can I ever begin to thank you, gentlemen!' he yarooped, grabbing the case from me. His top pocket lurched forward and swallowed it up. He glanced at his gold wrist-watch. 'Now, if you'll forgive me, gentlemen, I could go on chatting like this all day' —he motioned us towards the door we had only just entered— 'but I must return to my work. Most grateful indeed.'

As he motioned us out, a dreadful noise emerged from the door marked "SURGERY." It sounded as though a water-buffalo were breaking wind after being force-fed Lentil Surprise. It was followed by an equally dreadful clatter.

'Anyone else in the building with you, sir?' asked Holmes, getting straight to the point.

'It must be ... a kiwi fruit,' he replied, his old twitch reasserting itself.

Holmes raised an eyebrow, allowed it a quick flutter around his forehead, then lowered it back into place once again. 'You employ a kiwi fruit to oversee the washing-up, do you, sir? I believe they can be most effective,' he said, 'for all but the most stubborn household stains.'

'No, officer. I employ kiwi fruit only for purposes of experimentation. It is my area. I used to lead the world in testing cosmetics on animals; but there's little call for it now. I had to release two hundred and fifty rabbits back into the wild, all done up to the nines. Now, if you'll excuse me.'

The door closed firmly behind us, followed by the unmistakable sound of chains being re-hooked. Cautiously, I looked through the spy-hole once again; once again, another eye looked back. 'Mission accomplished,' I murmured to Holmes. 'Let us to the car.'

'B-b-but, sir!' exclaimed Holmes. 'We can't let him go without a bloody good bollocking! He's guilty as dammit, sir!'

'To the car, Holmes!' I thundered.

— · — · — · — · — · —

With Holmes's mutterings ringing in my ears, I drove approximately two hundred yards before taking a sharp right down a farm-track, ploughing through the odd sheep and lodging the car firmly behind a hedge. 'We will continue on foot, Holmes,' I said. 'Follow me!'

We charted an uncharted route across a muddy field. Mud! My feet have never enjoyed rubbing shoulders with mud, particularly mud as pushy and clingy as this. However hard I tried, I simply could not shake it off. But if life has taught me anything it is this: there comes a time when we must all slop through mud in order to arrive at a hideous bungalow.

At the far side of the field, we peered through a hedge into the garden at the rear of the Fellworthy lodging. There was little decoration in the garden, only a tree-like metallic washing-line, upon which what appeared to be fifty or sixty ear-muffs were blowing in the wind. But Holmes, it proved, had sharper eyes than I.

'Blimey, sir!' he gasped. 'Just look at 'em.'

'Who would want so many ear-muffs, Holmes? Is the man a pansy?'

'They're not ear-muffs, sir. They're ... hamsters.'

'Hamsters? What sort of monster would air his dead hamsters in public like that?'

'Who said anything about dead? Look, sir, lick your finger – there's no wind. Those hamsters are bloody *wriggling*!'

Personally, I have nothing whatsoever against the hamster community. But to crawl up a washing-line, prise open a peg and hang oneself out to dry struck me as the action of a half-wit.

'Shall we rescue 'em, sir?' hissed Holmes.

'Rescue them?'

'The hamsters, sir. My sister used to have one. Answered to the name of Sandy.'

'DC Holmes,' I said, pulling vigorously on my moustache. 'We are conducting a murder investigation. We are not Mr Steven McQueen on his scooter in *The Great Escape*. Look lively, man!'

At a pre-arranged sign – a kick in the shins – Holmes nipped under the hedge and across the lawn. He came to a halt by the north wall of the bungalow, crossed his hands and bent forward ready for me to join him. I took a running jump onto said hands and – whuuup! – pulled myself up onto the roof of the bungalow. I then leant over and, with great difficulty, helped Holmes up beside me.

A peek upwards while Fellworthy was making his lunge for the faux specs had alerted me to the fact that the bungalow was blessed with a skylight, running from one end of the roof to the other. Stealthily, Holmes and I now looked down through this skylight onto the strange scene below. Dr Fellworthy was sitting on the leather sofa in his sitting-room, bent over a long table, a solid if somewhat folksy affair constructed of oak and metal with a raffia inlay. Whenever he moved his head to the side, the glasses which

Mr Bates had gone to so much trouble to recreate would swing into our view beside their olive-green crushed Morocco case on the table. What was he doing with them? Did his intense interest in them mean that we had judged him unjustly, and that the fellow really did have an emotional yearning for their safe return?

Others might say that the Mortdecai heart is made of flint. I would deny it most strenuously. Flint indeed! Flint is far too fragile: granite, I think, is much more the material. But even my granite heart came close to breaking as I glimpsed the scene below me: the ageing doctor, pining for his deceased spouse, mournfully toying with his fondest memento of her. Glancing across the skylight at Holmes, I noticed that he, too, had a look of profound remorse skateboarding this way and that over his face. How could we have misjudged that poor medic so?

While Holmes's bulky sleeve gave chase to a runaway tear, Fellworthy walked out of the sitting-room, leaving the glasses and their case on the table. Seconds later, he returned with a plastic bag in one hand and a mallet in the other. Almost to our astonishment, he then placed the specs in the plastic bag, raised the mallet above his head, and with five well-placed blows, smashed them to smithereens. Without a second glance, he then transported the bag and its contents to a waste-paper basket, returned the mallet to its home, and poured himself a glass of Armagnac.

'Blimey, sir,' sighed Holmes. 'He took agin those specs, didn't he, sir? Would you say he's acting like a man who's got nothing to hide?'

'I fancy those hamsters could tell us a tale or two, Holmes. But I have a trick up my—'

'AND THERE IT SHALL REMAIN! HANDS IN THE AIR, GENTLEMEN!' An unfamiliar voice – half man, half woman, half speak-your-weight machine – barked behind us. We turned around, hands in the air. But the owner of the voice was all too familiar.

'Petal!' exclaimed Holmes. Before us stood the monstrous, huge-bosomed policewoman upon whom I had first set eyes in the cop-shop in Bucks. With a few wires attached and the odd burst of helium up her arse, she might have found more remunerative employment as a barrage-balloon. Performing a hand-stand on a grassy knoll in a city centre, she would have been a dead cert for an RIBA gold medal. But for the moment, she was pointing a double-barrelled shotgun at us.

'Petal, love, what are you doin' here?' Holmes spoke to her in one of those soft, kindly, caring voices that policemen reserve for overweight madwomen bearing shotguns. 'Come on, love, put that down, love, there must be some mistake, let's talk it over, you're suffering from stress, too much on your plate, think of the kiddies ...'

'Shut it, Holmes!' Petal bellowed back, giving him a hefty sock to the jaw with one of her spade-like hands. Holmes's face blew up something rotten. Within seconds, it looked as though a pair of fuller-figured jelly-fish were fornicating all over it.

'You shouldna done that, Petal,' winced the Detective Constable.

I seized the moment.

'Then you shouldn't have irritated the poor lady, Holmes. What did you expect? My sympathies are entirely with you, Petal, my poppet.' I knew how to deal with these bulldogs in a way that Holmes quite clearly did not. You either have it or you don't. To be frank, in all my dealings with women, I have always found that flattery can move she-mountains. 'And may I add, Petal, you look quite splendid in uniform, brandishing that gun so lustily, with the wind playing upon your hair like Neptune sifting with his trident through the very finest sea-weed.'

'You what?' she boomed. Her hand darted to my crotch like the claw of a mechanical digger. She then clutched my most prized possession and squeezed it until tears began spurting from my ears.

Without further ado, Petal kicked us off the roof of the bungalow. I landed face-first in a flower-bed, my poor moustache coated in clay. I barely had time to remonstrate before Petal was shinning down after us with the agility of a gorilla, but without the looks. 'March!' she boomed, pointing the gun at our backs and pushing us through the back door.

'Boots off!' she bellowed. I remembered the great store Dr Fellworthy set by personal cleanliness. 'The doctor is ready to see you now.' Clamped in her clammy clutch, we were paraded into the sitting-room before Dr Fellworthy, who was lovingly fingering a selection of hypodermic syringes.

'Ah, gentlemen! I see you have already met my assistant, Metal.'

'Petal,' Holmes corrected him.

'Wrong: Metal. Precious Metal. "Petal" is merely the pseudonym with which she has so successfully infiltrated the Police Force. You must take me for an imbecile! Precious Metal has been informing me of your incompetent meddling every step of the way. Call yourselves detectives? More like defectives!'

'Ha ha ha ha ha, sir! Ha ha ha ha ha, sir! Very good, sir. Very good.' Never had I seen Holmes more genuflective. Obsequiousness in others can be charming, but only when directed towards oneself. Directed towards Fellworthy, it was not a pretty sight.

'What are you doing, Holmes?' I hissed.

'Buying time, sir.'

'I'm afraid we have sold clean out,' said Fellworthy, glancing at his watch. 'Gentlemen, I was about to say, "Prepare to die." I believe that is the correct form. But there is no time for preparation. You must die first, and prepare yourselves later.'

Fellworthy drew a syringe with liquid of a most uncalled-for shade of pink and made ready to lunge. Facing death, my thoughts turned to the dearly beloved I would be leaving behind, principal among them my moustache. How would it get by without its dear Papa? One hears strong rumour that facial hair has mastered the trick of life after death, that it continues to sprout and blossom long after its hapless carrier has shuffled off his mortal coil. But life for a moustache in a coffin must be a pretty joyless affair. Inwardly, I cursed myself for having left no stipulation in my will for some sort of periscope arrangement, affording my moustache a glimpse of sunshine and rain, a glimpse of life carrying on as per u.

'Goodbye, sir! It's been a pleasure working with you, sir!' said Holmes, choking back his tears. I could barely bring myself to grunt a response. Holmes had proved himself unworthy of his position. He was simply not up to the job. This far on in the proceedings, Jock would have already unscrewed Fellworthy's head from his body and would even now be kicking it around the room for a little gratuitous footy practice. Where was the big ugly one, now that I needed him?

'Jock! Jock! JOCK!' I screamed at the top of my voice. I know what you're thinking. You're thinking that, in these life-and-death situations, it is more the done thing to shout, 'Mummy!' But then you never knew my mummy, did you?

In Petal's steely grip, I watched helpless, my upper lip playing havoc with the draughtsmanship of my foliage, as Fellworthy raised the syringe above his shoulder (a little melodramatically for my taste) and plunged it downwards –

'Yeeeeeehaaaaaaaarrrrrrrgggggghhhhh!'

– deep into Petal's arm. How could I have mistrusted Holmes so? With one swift karate chop, he had deftly re-directed the fatal needle.

'What the devil?' exclaimed Fellworthy, recovering himself and stabbing again with his syringe –

'Yooooooooooowwwwww!'

– deep into Petal's other arm.

'Don't worry, sir – I'll handle him!' With a swift high-kick which the most energetic member of the *Folies-Bergère* might have envied, Holmes caught Fellworthy on the jaw, and sent him skidding across the living-room, slap through that inelegant coffee table. 'Whoops, sorry, Doctor!' he cackled as his hand sharpened into a slicer. With an upward blow, he struck Fellworthy deep in the groin. A thwack to the knees with his truncheon ('Oh dear, pardon me, Doctor!') followed by a head-butt to the stomach ('Silly me! There I go again, Doctor!'), and Fellworthy was wriggling about on the parquet floor like the fidgetiest young maggot at a Montessori open day. Petal, on the other hand, was quite dead, the profile of her corpse taking me back down memory lane, to an exhausting walking holiday I once enjoyed in the Cairngorms.

'Lucky for us the doctor's so unsteady on his pins, eh, sir?' said Holmes with a chuckle.

'Luck does not come into it,' I snapped back a trifle tetchily.

I allowed myself a self-satisfied smile. It was only when my whiskers made contact with my eyebrows that it occurred to me that I might be overdoing it.

'Sometimes, my dear Holmes,' I added. 'It pays to remain calm.'

At that moment, Fellworthy's boot made forceful contact with my private parts and I was sent hurtling through the air, the wings of my moustache ensuring that my journey was smooth, even though the landing proved a mite bumpy.

It took a couple of discreet jabs to the windpipe from Holmes's little finger to bring Fellworthy back into line. At first, he was – how shall I put it? – a little delicate. But on awkward social occasions, I have always prided myself on getting the tongue-tied to, shall we say, open up. It's surprising how much magic may be worked using only a length of rope, a wooden chair, and the gentle wave of a lethal syringe.

'I loved Bronwen,' he moaned. 'Loved her, loved her, loved her.'

'You *loved* her?' I said. Easier to have loved an armadillo, I would have thought. But I kept my mouth shut.

'I begged her, *begged* her, to take me back, to give me another chance. She said it was either the kiwi fruit or her – she said I could not be married to both.'

'The kiwi fruit?'

'Genetic modification, you fool. It'll soon be all the rage. After the rabbits, I turned my attention to the kiwi. Why did no-one want to eat it any more? For a while, it had been the talk of the town. Kiwi this, kiwi that: they were selling like hot cakes. But then – nothing. I was contacted by the International Kiwi Association. They were desperate. Their research showed that consumers were turning to more convenient fruits such as the tangerine and the banana. They asked me to modify the kiwi to bring it more in line with consumer demands. After many false starts, I hit upon the idea of the Hamwi—'

'The Hamwi? What the hell is a Hamwi?'

'Half hamster, half kiwi, of course. The very first hamster-based fruit! It would walk off the shelves! And I was so very close to cracking it! The acclaim – the prestige – the honours – the money! But, oh no, Bronwen did *not* approve. I would have to choose. The kiwi or her. But I couldn't choose and if I couldn't have her, no-one else would! Collecting her car that day, I seized my chance: I rotated the lenses on her driving spectacles through ninety degrees. When she took to that wheel, it would have been like travelling on a rollercoaster upside down with her eyes crossed ...'

'You bowel fruit!' I exclaimed.

'What?'

'I meant, you foul brute! And what of your first wife?'

'Bronwen?'

'No, Doctor – Agnes.'

'Ah. Agnes. Dear Agnes. She died in a tragic motoring accident, as I recall ...'

'Let's not beat about the bush, Fellworthy,' I said, making pretty patterns in the air with my syringe. It seemed to do the trick.

'Agnes was well-insured and intensely irritating. A most hazardous combination, especially in marriage. Furthermore, she was epileptic. In the laboratory, I discovered how to induce an epileptic fit with a flicker-light oscillating at exactly the right frequency. For six months, I studied her every movement. She was a creature of habit, you see. She would always take the car at exactly 25mph down our drive. So I built a nice high fence with posts at just the right intervals, sent her out shopping one evening when the sun was bright but low – and ker-bang! The perfect crime!' Fellworthy emitted a triumphant smile.

I had heard enough. 'Perfect no more,' I commented. 'Even the General Medical Council might blanch at allowing a doctor to murder *both* his wives. Your evil has brought you only the prospect of prolonged incarceration in a urine-soaked cell with just a psychopathic sex-beast for company. But I can promise you this, Dr Fellworthy. If you come clean now, I may be able to secure you an upgrade in your accommodation. Club Class will ensure that your cell is soaked not with urine but with the great smell of Brut aftershave.'

'Not that! Anything but that!' stuttered the doctor.

'Very well,' I said, seizing my opportunity. 'If you don't tell me the truth, I shall guarantee that your cell will be doused in Brut aftershave three times a day, rising to four times on Sundays and Bank Holidays. Now, Doctor, spit it out – why did you murder Bronwen?'

'It was my hamsters – she took a shine to my hamsters – she hated the experimentation, hated it! But I was not going to have that woman stand between me and—'

'Tummy-rot!' I interjected. 'Baloney-balooney! You killed Bronwen because her research had led her to uncover the truth about you.'

'No – it was my hamsters! My beloved hamsters!'

'She had discovered there was a survivor of that massacre. A survivor not from the victims – but from their persecutors!'

'Hammy-hammy hamsters! She wanted to stop me playing with my hammy-hamsters!' Fellworthy was sobbing like a baby. I've never seen such a gush. If I had been of a more sporting inclination, I might have felt tempted to roll off his head in a barrel.

'Bugger the hammy-hamsters!' I said. 'You were the survivor, weren't you?'

'She never liked kiwi fruit anyway,' he blurted. 'Much preferred pineapple. I told her there was no future in pineapple, but would she listen? Would she?'

'She confronted you with her discovery. You made her promise she would never tell a soul, and that her research would cease forthwith. Nevertheless, you had those spectacles made just in case. And your foresight was rewarded, wasn't it? After your trip to Jersey, your marriage fell apart and it was then that you discovered that the research money was still flooding into her account. Having uncovered the truth, she could not let it go! Her desire for academic fame and glory was greater than any loyalty to you – and looking at you now, Doctor, one can only applaud her sense of priority!'

'You're wrong! You're wrong! She never approved of genetic modification! She was a vegetarian, near as dammit! Legs on her kiwi fruit – even small ones – would have upset her!'

'But you knew your Soviet masters would never have allowed this news to get out – they promised to kill you in some particularly excruciating fashion if you didn't stop her. So you chose your time carefully, reached for the novelty specs, and Bob's your uncle – she was gone!'

'Fruity little hamsters! Hammy little fruitsters!' he continued. I realised then that he was never going to come clean.

'It's the Brut-filled cell for you, my man. Excuse me while I step over Petal and call the Chief Constable. Do you know him? A Duke, of course. And one of the better ones.'

It must have been while my mind was floating back to the effortless superiority of his Grace that Fellworthy grabbed at his own skinny little moustache, pulled it clean off his face, hurled it into his mouth, swallowed it and perished in hideous agony right before our very eyes.

Holmes shook his head. 'Cyanide tablets hidden behind a false moustache,' he muttered, disapprovingly. 'The oldest trick in the book, eh, sir?'

'Which book?' I hissed.

XXI

Full house, kings on queens

Thanked be fortune, it has been otherwise
Twenty times better; but once in special,
In thin array after a pleasant guise,
When her loose gown from her shoulders did fall,
And she me caught in her arms long and small;
Therewithall sweetly did me kiss,
And softly said, dear heart, how like you this?

When Jock spotted me across the concourse at Jersey airport his great, battered face contorted itself into a frightful snarl, causing innocent bystanders to scatter like sheep and huddle in corners, clutching their infants. I well knew that this one-fanged grimace was meant as a cheery grin but it still never fails to frighten even me. The effect was enhanced by the black patch over the empty eye-socket. As I approached he remembered that I have often told him not to wear such a patch when women and children are about; there were stifled shrieks from the terrified populace as he tore it off, fished his glass eye out of a trouser pocket, spat on it and rammed it home. Back to front.

'Nice to see you, Mr Charlie,' he growled.

'And it is nice to see your honest face, Jock, as refreshing as a glass of cool water.'

'You got a bloody lovely memory, Mr Charlie.'

'Eh?'

'I mean, fancy you remembering what cold water tastes like.' And he unleashed the grin again.

The journey home was uneventful, if you call it uneventful to be jounced about in a Rolls driven at 70 mph through the narrow, winding lanes of an island whose speed limit is 40.

'That excrement on your mush is growing away nice, Mr Charlie.'

'Thank you. Arising out of that, how are the canary's bowels?'

'Oh, he's back in top form, passing lovely little motions, regular as clockwork. I put him back on the red pepper and rum diet, always works the oracle. I sometimes reckon he holds back on purpose, just to get his grog.'

'Well, go steady with it: I'm not having drunken canaries cursing and belching and trolling dirty songs when the Rector calls.'

'Yeah. Did you find out who clobbered the schoolmarm and that?'

'Yes, thanks.'

'Get bashed up much?'

'Once or twice. People never seem to tire of beating me about the head.'

'Arr,' he said enigmatically.

'Madam at home?'

'Yeah. Come back yesdee. Her and Cookie are making you a special surprise dinner for tonight.' I raised a mental eyebrow – this did not sound like the sullen virago who had sped me to Oxford unkist.

Indeed, as I decanted myself from the car it was a smiling, loving wife who ran to greet me, taking my hands in hers and devouring my face – except for the moustached area – with huge, brimming eyes.

'Oh, Charlie Charlie Charlie!' she cried, as is her wont.

'There there there,' I said gruffly, folding her into my arms but taking care that our faces should be side-by-side rather than vis-à-vis, for obvious reasons. Soon I was in my personal armchair, my favourite blue velvet smoking-jacket and a matching pair of Morocco slippers, beaming at the glass of brandy which, with her own hands, she had placed within my easy reach.

'Tell me all about it,' she urged. I told all of it that was fit for her gently-nurtured ears. Agog is what she was as she drank in the narrative. It was evident to the trained eye that she lov'd me for the dangers I had pass'd and I lov'd her that she did pity them.

'And how was S. Tropez?' I asked. 'Did you have fun?' She levelled the aforementioned huge eyes at me again – and once again they were brimming with many a happy tear.

'Oh, Charlie dearest, I meant to be unfaithful to you, out of spite I guess, but when it came to the crunch I just couldn't. Anyway, all the men were so lean and muscular and bronzed and, well, I guess I've kind of got used to a cuddly guy. Oh, Charlie darling, I'd love to cuddle up with you right this moment and smother you with burning kisses and eat you all up, every scrap.'

She lowered her splendid eyelashes demurely.

'Well, what are we waiting for?' I murmured. 'I see no obstacle to such a course.' She did not answer, but a shadow passed over her face and she flicked a reproachful glance at the hedge-like obstacle. In an instant the moustache and my libido were locked in a death-struggle, a desperate battle of wills. The former was hopelessly outclassed, of course; no moustachio has ever won such a contest, the Old Adam is always victorious. Soon I had that moustache on its knees, whining for mercy, pleading that it was too young to die. But I was Adamant.

'No quarter!' I said, sternly.

'How do you mean, Charlie dear?' asked Johanna, knitting her lovely brows.

'Never mind. Just press the bell for Jock, please.'

'Jock,' I said when he entered, 'is there plenty of hot water? Good. Is there a stout pair of scissors in the bathroom? And a razor and my larger badger-hair shaving-brush?' His eyes seemed to sparkle; it was the eye of a man who scarcely dares hope – a thug who cannot believe the witness of his cauliflower ear.

'Yes, Jock, you have guessed aright. I intend to prune this floribunda right back to its parent lip. I shall raze it to the ground, leaving not a wrack behind. *Cartago delenda est!*'

'Right, Mr Charlie,' he said in hushed tones. 'Want any help?'

'No, Jock. I appreciate your offer but there are some things a sahib has to face alone.'

Johanna and I fled upstairs hand in hand and soon I was standing before the mirror, looking my last on Tiger Clemenceau – and at Johanna's reflection in the glass as she slithered out of her costly raiment in a way which sent my blood-pressure right up into the paint-cards. Twice I raised the glittering executioner's blade to my upper lip and twice it fell from my nerveless fingers. Johanna stole up to me and nibbled lovingly in my ear.

'Infirm of purpose,' she murmured. 'Give me the scissors.'

I believe it was on the following Monday that I was sitting in the kitchen, munching my elevenses and exchanging civilities with the canary.

'Shaving the upper lip,' I remarked, 'is a curse which canaries and women have been spared.' It cocked its ear. 'Except of course, certain aunts,' I added, evoking a squawk of alarm from the feathered f.

'On the other hand,' I mused, fondling the bare ruined choir where once the sweet-briar sprang, 'you and they will never know the bliss of being freshly shaven.'

Jock brought in the mail. Continuing to munch, I picked out of the bundle one of those big, costly envelopes such as only American Embassies can nowadays afford. The contents read as follows, to wit:

> *Sir,*
>
> *I am directed to require you, immediately on receipt of this letter, to return the Temporary Accreditation Wallet issued to you by the undersigned.*
>
> *This return should be made by hand of officer or, failing that, by British Registered Mail.*

I am further directed to express the thanks of the Section concerned of the Department concerned for your friendly co-operation in the recent academic research. That Section is given to understand that if at any time in the future you should be in Washington, DC and cared to sign the Visitor's Book in the Guard Room of the White House, you would receive an invitation to join the President and the First Lady at the Cocktail Hour.

'You all right, Mr Charlie?' asked Jock crossly.

'Yes, Jock. Sorry, just giggling.'

'Well, you're upsetting the canary, aren't you. You know what his bowels are like.'

'Yes,' I said, continuing to read.

You will appreciate that only subjects of general and unspecific interest are discussed at the Cocktail Hour.

Cordially,
  H. Blucher
  Colonel, US Army

P.S. Hey Charlie, you old sod, you know that doctor who did an auto-destruct while you waited? We ran the usual routine checks and, would you believe it, your Special Branch had a file on him. He emigrated to Britain in 1946; naturalised 1948, changed name by deed poll 1949. Original name: Nikolai Djugashvili Ulianov. How about that?

I stared at the words. 'Yeah,' I said, turning to the canary. 'How *about* that, hunh?'

It shrugged its shoulders and went on catching the crumbs from my bacon sandwich.

KYRIL BONFIGLIOLI

THE MORTDECAI NOVELS

"I am Charlie Mortdecai. I like art and money and dirty jokes and drink. I am very successful."

Don't Point That Thing at Me
The Hon. Charlie Mortdecai is up to his earlobes in trouble. A Goya painting has gone missing and the authorities seem to think he knows something about it. He does. If he and his thuggish manservant Jock are not very careful, some very nasty men with guns are liable to make them very dead.

After You With the Pistol
It's been made clear to Charlie that he has to marry the beautiful, sex-crazed and very rich Johanna Krampf. The only fly in the ointment is that she seems determined to involve him in her crazy schemes of monarch-assassination and heroin smuggling. Perhaps it's all in a good cause—if only he can live long enough to find out.

Something Nasty in the Woodshed
Charlie has decamped to Jersey after a spot of bother in London, and is hoping to lie low with his manservant and his new bride. But then a friend's wife is attacked, and for once he takes on the role of pursuer rather than pursued.

All the Tea in China
After an act of lechery that anyone but a close relative might forgive, Karli Mortdecai Van Cleef, a distant relative of the Hon. Charlie Mortdecai, throws in his lot with an opium clipper bound for China. So begins a staggering adventure. It runs in the family . . .

All available from The Overlook Press

www.overlookpress.com